DOCTOR WHO AND THE
HORROR OF FANG ROCK

DOCTOR WHO
AND THE HORROR
OF FANG ROCK

Based on the BBC television serial *The Horror of Fang Rock* by Terrance Dicks by arrangement with the British Broadcasting Corporation

TERRANCE DICKS

published by
the Paperback Division of
W. H. Allen & Co. Ltd.

A Target Book

Published in 1978
by the Paperback Division of W. H. Allen & Co. Ltd.
A Howard & Wyndham Company
44 Hill Street, London W1X 8LB

Text of book copyright © 1978 by Terrance Dicks
'Doctor Who' series copyright © 1978 by the
British Broadcasting Corporation

Printed in Great Britain by
Richard Clay (The Chaucer Press) Ltd, Bungay, Suffolk

ISBN 0 426 20009 3

Contents

Prologue

The Legend of Fang Rock

Fang Rock lighthouse, centre of a series of mysterious and terrifying events at the turn of the century, is built on a rocky island a few miles off the Channel coast. So small is the island that wherever you stand its rocks are wet with sea-spray. Everywhere you hear the endless thundering of the waves, as they crash on the jagged coastline that has given Fang Rock its name.

The lighthouse tower is in the centre of the island. A steep flight of steps leads up to the heavy door in its base. This gives entry to the lower floor where the big steam-driven generator throbs steadily away, providing power for the electric lantern. Coal bunkers occupy the rest of this lower area.

Winding stairs lead up to the crew room, where the men eat, sleep and spend most of their leisure time. Next to the crew room is a tiny kitchen.

Above, more store rooms and the head keeper's private cabin, and above them the service rooms, where tools and spare parts are kept, together with rockets, maroons, flares and a variety of other warning devices.

Finally, a short steep iron stairway leads up into the lamp room, a glassed-in circular chamber at the very top of the tower, dominated by the giant carbon-arc lamp with its gleaming glass prisms.

Fang Rock has had an evil reputation from its earliest days. Soon after it was built two men died in mysterious circumstances, and a third went mad with fear. There have been strange rumours, stories of a great glowing beast that comes out of the sea . . .

But all that is forgotten now. It is the early 1900s, and the age of science is in full swing. Newly converted from oil to electricity, Fang Rock lighthouse stands tall and strong, the great shining lantern warning ships away from the jagged reefs around the little island.

As night falls one fine autumn evening the lamp is burning steadily. The three men who make up the crew go peacefully about their duties, unaware of the night of horror that lies before them, little knowing that they would soon be caught up in a strange and terrible conflict, with the fate of the Earth itself as the final stake.

The Terror Begins

It began with a light in the sky. It was dusk, and the lamp had just been lit. High up in the lamp room all was calm and peaceful, no sound except for the steady roar of the sea below. Young Vince saw it first. He was polishing the great telescope on the lamp-room gallery when he saw a fiery streak blazing across the darkness. Through the telescope, he tracked its progress as it curved down through the evening sky and into the sea. For a moment the sea glowed brightly at the point of impact. The glow faded, and everything was normal.

Vince turned away from the telescope. 'Reuben! Come and look—quick now!'

With his usual aggravating deliberation the old man finished filling an oil-lamp. 'What is it now, boy?'

'There was this light, shot across the sky. Went under the sea it did, and the sea was all glowing. Over there.'

Old Reuben rose stiffly, hobbled across to the telescope and peered through the eyepiece. 'Nothing there now.'

'I told you, it went into the sea.'

Reuben grunted. 'Could have been a what d'you call 'em . . . a meteor . . .'

He left the telescope and Vince took his place, scanning the area of sea where the fireball had vanished. 'Whatever it was it come down pretty near us . . .'

'Sight-seeing are we?' asked a sarcastic voice. 'Hoping to spot some of them bathing belles on the beach?'

Guiltily Vince jumped away from the telescope. Ben Travers, senior keeper and engineer of Fang Rock lighthouse, was regarding him sardonically from the doorway. He was a tough, weathered man in his fifties, stern-faced but not without his own dour humour.

Reuben chuckled. 'Young Vince here's been seeing stars.'

Vince reddened under Ben's sceptical stare. 'I saw a light, anyway. Clear across the sky it came, and down into into the sea.'

'Must have been a shooting star, eh?'

'Weren't no shooting star,' said Vince obstinately. 'Seen them before I have. This was—different.'

'Get on with you,' cackled Reuben. 'That were a shooting star, right enough. Bring you luck, boy, that will. Bit of luck coming to you.'

'What, on this old rock? Not till my three months is up!' Keepers worked three months at a stretch, followed by an off-duty month on shore.

Ben went to the telescope. But there was nothing to be seen but the steady swell of the sea. 'Well, whatever it was it's gone now. As long as it's not a hazard to navigation, it's no business of ours.'

That's Ben for you, thought Vince. Duty first, last and all the time. 'I saw it, though,' he persisted. 'It was all glowing . . .'

'I've heard enough about it, lad. Just you forget it and get on with your work. I'm going down to supper. Coming, Reuben?'

Ben went down the steps, and Reuben followed. Vince returned to polishing the brass mounting of the telescope. He stared out at the dark, rolling sea. 'All the same,' he muttered, 'I know what I saw . . .'

It surfaced from the depths of the sea and scanned the surrounding area with many-faceted eyes. Just ahead was a small, jagged land mass. Crowning it was a tall slender tower with a light on top that flashed at regular intervals. Clearly there were intelligent life-forms on the island. They must be studied, and eventually disposed of, it thought weakly.

It had been severely shaken by the crash, and its energy-levels were dangerously low. The bright flashing light meant power—and it desperately needed power to restore its failing strength. It had already taken precautionary measures to conceal its presence and isolate the island. Slowly it moved through the sea towards the lighthouse.

In the cosy, familiar warmth of the crew room Ben and Reuben were dealing with plates of stew, and continuing their never-ending argument.

Reuben swallowed a mouthful of dumpling. 'Now in the old days it was all simple enough. You filled her up and trimmed the wick. That old lamp just went on burning away steady as you please.'

'Wasn't only the lamp burned sometimes. How many oil fires were there in those days, eh? Towers gutted, men killed . . .'

'Carelessness, that is. Carelessness, or drink. Oil's safe enough if you treat her right.'

'Listen, Reuben, I've been inside a few of those old lighthouses. Like the inside of a chimney. Grease and soot everywhere, floor covered with oil and bits of wick.'

'Never, mate, never!'

Ben was well into his stride by now. 'And as for the light! You couldn't see it inside, let alone out. Clouds of black smoke as soon as the lamp was lit.'

Reuben changed his ground. 'All right, then, if electricity's so good, why are they going back to oil then, tell me that?'

Ben groaned. They'd been over this hundreds of times, but Reuben couldn't—or wouldn't—understand. 'That's an oil-vapour system, different thing altogether. They reckon it's cheaper.'

'Well of course it's cheaper,' grumbled Reuben. 'By the time you've ferried out all that coal for your generators . . .'

There was a whistle from the speaking-tube on the wall. Reuben got up, unhooked the receiver and bellowed, 'Ahoy!'

Vince snatched his ear from the receiver and winced. Reuben always bellowed so loud he hardly needed the tube. He put the tube to his lips and said, 'That you, Reuben?'

He held the tube to his ear and grinned at the reply that sizzled from the tube. 'Oh, it's King Edward himself, is it? Well, your majesty, be kind enough to tell the principal keeper as there's a fog coming up like nobody's business.' His voice became more serious. 'Funny looking fog it is too. I never seen anything like it.'

Reuben replaced the speaking-tube. 'Vince says there's a fog coming up.'

'Fog? There was no sign earlier.'

'He reckons it's a thick un, Ben. Something funny about it.'

Ben pushed his plate back. 'Best go and see for myself. Boy's only learning, after all.'

He hurried out of the room. Reuben mopped up

the last of his stew with a hunk of bread, stuffed it into his mouth and followed him.

Ben stared out of the gallery, shaking his head. 'Never seen a fog come up so fast—and so thick!'

The fog seemed to be rising straight from the surface of the sea like steam. It surged and billowed round the lighthouse, isolating it in a belt of swirling grey cloud.

Reuben looked out into the grey nothingness. 'Terrible thing, fog,' he said with gloomy relish. 'Worst thing for sailors there ever was.'

Ben shivered. 'And feel that cold. Coming right across from Iceland that, I reckon.'

'It's coming from where I saw that thing go into the sea,' said Vince.

Ben rounded on him irritably. 'Give over, boy. Go and start the siren going.'

Unexpectedly, Reuben came to Vince's support. 'He might be right though, Ben. It do seem unnatural, this fog, coming up so sudden like. I never seen anything like it.'

'Not you too,' said Ben wearily. He nodded to Vince. 'Well, get on with it, boy. Frequent blasts on the foghorn—and I *do* mean frequent.'

Reuben couldn't resist trying to score a point. 'Pity we're not still using oil. Everyone knows an oil-lamp gives better light in fog.'

As always Ben rose to the bait. 'Rubbish, that's

just an old wives' tale. Electricity's just as good in fog, and a sight more reliable.'

The lamp went out.

Reuben gave a satisfied cackle. The timing was perfect. 'You was saying something about reliability, Ben,' he said with heavy irony.

Ben grabbed an oil-lamp, lit it and ran from the lamp room.

On the other side of the tiny island there was a wheezing groaning sound and a square blue shape materialised out of the fog. It was a blue London Police Box. Out of it stepped a tall man with wide inquisitive eyes and a tangle of curly hair. He wore loose comfortable clothes, a battered soft hat and a long trailing scarf. He was followed by a dark-eyed, brown-haired girl in Victorian clothes. The man was that mysterious traveller in Space and Time known as the Doctor, and his companion was a girl called Leela.

Leela looked round at the wet rocks and swirling fog. She shivered. 'You said I'd like Brighton. Well, I don't.'

'Does this look like Brighton?' asked the Doctor exasperatedly.

'How do I know? I don't know what Brighton's supposed to look like.'

'It isn't even Hove,' mused the Doctor. 'Could be Worthing, I suppose . . .'

Leela looked at the Police Box—in reality a Space/Time craft called the TARDIS. 'The machine has failed again?'

'No, not really,' said the Doctor defensively. 'Not *failed*, exactly. It's still the right planet, and I'm pretty sure we're still in the same time-zone—though we may have jumped forward a year or two. We're even in the right general area—assuming this is Worthing, of course.'

'You can't tell!' accused Leela. 'What's gone wrong?'

The Doctor cleared his throat. 'Well, you see, a localised condition of planetary atmospheric condensation caused a malfunction in the visual orientation circuits, or to put it another way, we got lost in the fog!'

He took a few paces around the rocks and paused in surprise. The sea winds had cleared the fog for a second or two, and he caught a glimpse of a tall thin shape towering above them. 'How very strange!'

'What is?'

'A lighthouse—without a light!'

Holding his oil-lamp high above his head, Ben hurried into the big generator room that occupied the whole of the base of the tower. The generator was still chugging busily away. It should have been producing power—but it wasn't. Puzzled, he went to examine the power feed lines. Perhaps a faulty connection . . . The electric lights came on again.

Ben looked at the throbbing generator. Although he'd never admit it to Reuben, electrical science was still in its infancy, and puzzling things like this still cropped up occasionally. Something in the atmosphere perhaps. Something to do with this strange fog.

With a last puzzled look at the generator, Ben turned and began to climb the stairs. As he left the room, the door to the coal storage bunker opened a fraction. There was a glow, and a faint crackling sound . . .

As the light came on again, Vince turned triumphantly to Reuben. 'There, that didn't take long, did it?'

Reuben scowled. A major power failure would have been a big point on his side. 'Working, not working, working again! Never know where you are with it, do you?'

Vince shivered and slapped his arms across his chest. 'Perishing up here. I'll just go down and get my sweater.'

'You do that, boy, and bring mine up as well.'

Vince ran down the stairs, bumping into Ben on the landing. 'Come down for my sweater,' he explained. 'Freezing up there it is.'

Ben followed him into the crew room. 'Same in the generator room, even with the boilers.'

Vince went to his sea-chest, pulled out a heavy

fisherman's jersey, and began pulling it over his head. 'Didn't take you long to repair her, though.'

Ben went over to his desk and took the log book from its drawer. 'I did nothing. Came on by herself.' He took pen and ink out of the drawer and opened the log book.

Vince stared at him. 'Came on by herself? What, for no reason?'

'It's got me fair flummoxed, Vince. There's something going on here tonight. Something I don't understand.'

He started writing in the log in his laborious copperplate, then paused and looked up. 'You and Reuben find all the oil-lamps you can get hold of and fill 'em up. I want several in every room—and one left burning. If the power goes again we won't be in the dark.'

The Doctor and Leela were working their way over slippery wet rocks towards the lighthouse. They were very near the coastline and Leela shook herself like a cat as a particularly violent shower of spray drenched her to the skin. She saw a light shining high above them. 'Look, Doctor!'

'Good. We'll just knock on the door and get directions and a date and be on our way. Once I know our exact Time-Space Co-ordinates . . .'

Leela jumped again, as a low booming note came through the fog. 'What was that? A sea beast?' She felt for her knife, then remembered, the Doctor wouldn't let her wear it with these clothes.

'It's only a foghorn,' said the Doctor reassuringly. 'It's to warn ships to stay away from these rocks. They might not spot the light in this fog.'

Leela stood still, poised, staring intently into the fog.

The Doctor said impatiently, 'Come on, Leela, you know what ships are? You saw some on the Thames, remember?'

The Doctor had first met Leela in the future on a faraway planet. She was a descendant of a planetary survey team that had become marooned. Over the years they had degenerated into the Sevateem, a tribe of extremely warlike savages, and Leela had been one of their fiercest warriors. Her travels with the Doctor had civilised her a little—but she reverted to the primitive immediately when there was any hint of trouble.

Part of Leela's savage inheritance was a kind of sixth sense that alerted her to the presence of danger. It was clear from the expression on her face that this instinct was in operation now. 'There is something wrong here, Doctor. Something dangerous and evil. I can feel it . . .'

Vince filled another oil-lamp, lit it and set it to one side. 'Old Ben's really worried!'

Reuben's head emerged tortoise-like from the

neck of his sweater. 'So he should be, boy. Him and his precious electricity. I told him often enough . . .'

'Writing it all down in the log he is. Says he can't understand it.'

The electric lights went out again. The two men looked at each other.

Reuben was triumphant. 'Done it again, see?'

Vince shook his head. 'Poor old Ben. He'll be spitting blood, won't he?'

Lantern in hand, Ben hurtled down the stairs at a dangerous speed, and arrived panting in the generator room. Once again the generator was chugging merrily away, with nothing to explain the total loss of power. 'Not again,' he muttered. 'I don't believe it! Makes no flaming sense . . .' He began checking over the generator.

There was a shattering crash behind him as the door to the coal bunker was flung open with tremendous force. Ben spun round, and his face twisted with horror at the hideous sight before him.

In his terror he dropped his lantern. The generator room was plunged into darkness, illuminated only by the glow of the thing in the doorway.

There was a faint crackling sound as it flowed towards him. Ben screamed with terror . . .

2

Strange Visitors

The melancholy boom of the siren drowned the sound of Ben's dying scream.

Vince released the handle and took out his watch. 'She's been off over two minutes this time.'

Reuben nodded gloomily. 'She'll not come back on again so quick this time.'

Vince shrugged. 'Don't make a lot of difference, do it, not in this fog. A ship'd have her bows right on Fang Rock before they'd see our old lamp in this.'

Reuben stared out into the night. There was nothing to be seen but grey swirling fog. 'It's a queer do, this fog. No cause for it.'

Vince tried to remember the scientific principles Ben had taught him. 'Cold air and warm air mixing. That's what causes fog.'

Reuben snorted. 'I've been thirty year in the service, Vince. One look at the sky and I know when fog's coming. And today was clear as clear. It isn't natural . . .'

Uneasily Vince said, 'Maybe I'd best go down, see if Ben needs a hand.'

'Aye, you do that, lad.' As Vince moved away the old man repeated softly, 'It isn't natural . . .'

The Doctor and Leela reached the lighthouse at last and climbed the steps. The Doctor pounded on the heavy wooden door. 'Keeper! Keeper!' There was no reply. He shoved at the door and it creaked slowly open.

They stood on the threshold of the generator room, peering into semi-darkness. The room was lit only by the faint glow from the boiler fire. The Doctor listened to the steady throbbing of the machinery. 'The generator seems to be working—so why isn't there any power?'

'I'm not a Tesh——' Leela paused, correcting herself. 'I mean a—Teshnician!'

The Doctor peered at the generator. 'Could be shorting out somewhere I suppose . . .'

Leela could see him mentally rolling up his sleeves. 'And I suppose you're going to mend it?'

A little guiltily, the Doctor stepped back. 'What, without permission? Wouldn't dream of it! We'd better find the crew—this way, I think.'

They crossed the room and began climbing the stairs. 'Teshnician, where are you?' called the Doctor. 'Hullo, anybody there?'

A light bobbed down towards them and a scared voice called, 'That you, Ben?'

'No, it isn't.'

They rounded the curve of stairs on to the landing and saw a thin young man in a fisherman's sweater. He was clutching an oil-lamp and was obviously very frightened. He stared at the Doctor and Leela in sheer disbelief. 'Here . . . who are you then?'

'I'm the Doctor, and this is Leela. You seem to be having some trouble.'

'How'd you get here?'

'We came in the TARDIS,' explained Leela helpfully.

Before she could go into more detail the Doctor said hurriedly, 'We're mislaid mariners. Our . . . craft is moored on the other side of the island.'

Vince nodded, reassured. Funny name, TARDIS, but then, lots of people gave their boats fancy foreign names. 'Got lost in the fog, did you? You'd best come into the crewroom.'

As he led them inside he asked, 'Where are you making for?'

Leela gave the Doctor a look and said, 'Brighton!'

Vince laughed. 'Well, well, you did get lost then, didn't you?'

He began lighting oil-lamps, filling the room with their warm yellow glow.

The Doctor looked round. Except for its semi-circular shape the room was much like the main cabin of a ship. Bunks lined the walls, there were chests and lockers, and a litter of personal possessions. There was a table in the centre of the room. Against the wall stood an old wooden desk, and a smaller table with a wireless telegraph apparatus.

Vince bustled about, offering them chairs. He was nervous and chatty, obviously glad of company. 'I'll get you some hot food, soon as we're sorted out.

23

You'll not want to put to sea again in this. This TARDIS of yours, small craft is she?'

'Yes,' said the Doctor.

'No,' said Leela.

Vince stared at them.

'Big in some ways, small in others,' the Doctor explained hastily. 'Now then, what's the trouble here?'

'Generator keeps playing up, sir. Lights go off then come on again, for no reason.'

The Doctor nodded thoughtfully. 'Tricky things, some of these early generators.'

'Ours isn't an early one, sir. It's the latest modern design. Driving Ben wild though, all the same.'

'Ben?'

'He's the engineer, sir.'

'Are there just the two of you?'

'Three, sir. Old Reuben's still up in the lamp room. Fit to bust, he is. Fair killing himself.'

Leela was puzzled. 'He is under a spell?'

Vince gave her a look. 'What I mean is, he's one of the old-fashioned sort, see? Hates electricity. Never been happy since they took out the oil.'

The Doctor smiled. 'I know the type. In the early days of oil he'd have been saying there was nothing like a really large candle!'

'That's old Reuben right enough!'

'Where's your engineer now? I should have

24

thought he would have been working on the generator.'

'But he is, sir. You must have seen him when you came in.'

'No, I didn't.'

'He'll have stepped out for a moment then. You missed him in the fog.'

'No,' said Leela definitely. 'If anyone had been near I would have heard them.'

Vince looked utterly baffled. 'Suppose I'd better go and look for him then.' It was clear he didn't have much enthusiasm for the task.

'That's all right,' said the Doctor. 'Tell you what——' he paused. 'What's your name?'

'Vince, sir. Vince Hawkins.'

'I'll go and look for your engineer, Mr Hawkins. As a matter of fact I'm something of an engineer myself. Perhaps I can give him a hand. You look after the young lady.'

There was a note of authority in the Doctor's voice and Vince said meekly, 'Right you are, sir.'

The Doctor went down the stairs and Vince smiled shyly at Leela. 'This is quite a treat for me, miss.'

'Is it?' Leela gave him a puzzled look and wandered over to the telegraph, idly lifting the brass key and letting it fall.

'Don't touch that please, miss,' said Vince apologetically. 'Ben's pride and joy, that is. No one else is allowed to handle it.' Leela moved away from the telegraph and Vince went on. 'It's a lonely life on the lighthouse you see. Sometimes I go out and talk to the seals, just for a change from Reuben and Ben.'

'Seals are animals. Sea creatures?'

'That's right, miss.'

'Then it is stupid to talk to them. You should listen to the old ones of your tribe, it is the only way to learn.'

Vince sighed. 'I'll get you some food and a hot drink, miss.'

Leela tugged ruefully at her wet dress. 'I need some dry clothes more than anything else.'

'I'm afraid we don't have anything suitable for a lady,' began Vince.

'I'm not a lady, Vince,' said Leela calmly. She eyed him thoughtfully. 'We are much of a size. Clothes such as you wear will be quite suitable for me.'

Vince looked down at his fisherman's trousers and sweater. 'But these are men's things, miss, working clothes . . .'

He broke off, gasping. Leela had unbuttoned her wet dress and was calmly stepping out of it. 'That's my clothes-chest over there, miss, just you help yourself. I'll get you that hot food.' He turned and almost ran into the kitchen.

As she struggled out of the wet skirt, Leela stared after him in puzzlement. There was no doubt about it, these Earth people were very strange . . .

The Doctor gazed into the darkness of the generator

room. 'Anyone here?' he called. 'Ben? Ben?'

No answer. The Doctor crossed the room, passing the still-throbbing generator, and opened the out-side door. A blast of icy air, mixed with fog, swirled into the room. The Doctor called out into the night. 'Ben? Ben, are you there?' Still no answer. Only the thunder of the waves on the nearby rocks. Puzzled, the Doctor closed the door—and the lights came on.

The Doctor rubbed his chin. 'Curiouser and curi-ouser!' He began walking round the generator, ex-amining it more closely. The brightness of the electric lamps had dispelled the shadows behind it, and now the Doctor saw a huddled shape lying against the wall. He knelt to examine it, just as Vince came in, and looked round the brightly-lit room in astonish-ment. 'Well done, sir. You are an engineer and no mistake.' Suddenly Vince realised that the Doctor was nowhere in sight. 'Doctor, where are you?'

The Doctor appeared from behind the generator. 'Over here.'

'You managed to find the trouble, then?'

'I always find trouble,' said the Doctor sombrely.

Vince looked uneasily at him, sensing the strange-ness of his manner. 'Ben'll be pleased.'

'I doubt it.'

Leela came into the room. She was wearing Vince's best pair of boots and one of his spare jerseys, and buckling the belt on his best shore-going trousers.

'Oh Ben'll be pleased right enough, sir,' said Vince. 'He couldn't make head nor tail of what was wrong.

I wonder where he's got to?'

The Doctor pointed to the shape behind the generator. 'Ben's down here. He's been dead for some time.'

Vince rushed over to the body. 'Ben!' he gasped. 'Oh Ben, no . . . no . . .' His voice trailed away.

'What killed him, Doctor?' asked Leela practically.

'As far as I can tell, a massive electric shock. He must have died instantly.'

Vince looked up. 'The generator, you mean? But he was always so careful.'

Leela looked at the throbbing machine. 'It was dark . . .'

'He had a lantern, though.' Vince rubbed a hand over his eyes. 'I just can't believe this has happened.'

Gently the Doctor helped him to his feet. 'Vince, hadn't you better go and tell Reuben?'

Vince nodded wearily. 'Yes sir.' He stumbled away.

The Doctor looked at the body, and Leela looked at the Doctor. 'You do not believe he was killed by the machine?'

'No.'

'Then what——'

The Doctor put a finger to his lips and crept silently over to the coal store. He picked up a heavy shovel and nodded to Leela. She flung open the door . . . but there was nothing there except coal.

The Doctor threw down the shovel. 'I thought perhaps there was something nasty in the coal shed, but

28

apparently not.' He shut the door. 'But there's something very nasty somewhere on this island.'

'A sea creature?'

The Doctor was prowling restlessly about. 'If it is, it's a most unusual one. It opens and shuts doors, comes and goes without so much as a wet footprint, and has a mysterious ability to interfere with electrical power.' He kneeled by Ben's body and examined it once more. He saw that there was something caught beneath it, and dragged it free.

'What have you found, Doctor?'

'Ben's lantern,' said the Doctor slowly. He held it up. The heavy metal frame was melted, warped, twisted, like candle wax in the heat of a furnace. The Doctor handed it to Leela. 'What kind of sea creature could do a thing like that?'

3

Shipwreck

Reuben listened to the news of Ben's death in stunned silence. When Vince had finished, the old man said slowly, 'Ben knew every inch of that machine. Don't make sense, boy, him dying like that.'

'That's what happened, according to the Doctor. Massive electric shock, he said.'

'This Doctor—foreigner is he?'

'Don't think so. Young lady speaks a bit strange like, though. Why?'

'Spies!' said Reuben dramatically.

Vince smiled, despite his grief. 'Spies? What'd spies be doing on Fang Rock?'

'There's Frogs,' said Reuben. 'And Ruskies. Germans too. Can't trust none of 'em.'

'These two ain't spies, Reuben.'

'Well, all this trouble started just about the time they got here. Don't forget that!'

'You ain't saying *they* might have done for Ben?'

Pleased with the effect of his words Reuben said solemnly, 'I'm saying there's strange doings here tonight, and for all we know them two strangers are at the bottom of it. Reckon I best go down and keep an eye on 'em.'

Vince didn't know what to think. His instinct was to trust the Doctor, but what Reuben had said was true enough. Another thought struck him. 'Here, Reuben, you'll have to send a message to the shore station. We need a relief engineer—and the boat can take Ben away . . .'

'I'll see to it soon as it's light. Where is he?'

'Generator room. I know it don't seem respectful. But it's only till the boat comes . . .'

Reuben lowered his voice. 'He won't rest easy, you know, lad!'

'What do you mean?' stammered Vince.

'If he was killed by that machine there'll be anger in his soul. Men who die like that don't never rest easy!'

Reuben stumped off. Vince stood alone in the lamp room. The events of the last few hours suddenly closed in on him and he began shaking with fear.

The Doctor was examining the telegraph apparatus when Reuben came into the crew room.

'Very interesting this, Leela—a fine example of an early Marconi wireless telegraph.'

'Leave that be, sir, if you don't mind,' said Reuben sharply.

The Doctor turned. 'You'll be Reuben I take it. Shouldn't you be using this telegraph to report your engineer's death?'

'Wireless won't bring Ben back. I'll semaphore in the morning, when the fog clears.'

'You do know how to use the telegraph?'

' 'Course I do, we all does. But Ben was the expert. I'll use the semaphore tomorrow.'

The Doctor nodded understandingly, guessing that the old man had only the vaguest idea how to work the device, but was too obstinate to admit it.

Reuben stripped a blanket from a bunk and folded it over his arm. Leela touched it curiously, but he snatched it away.

'You leave that alone, miss.'

'What is it for?'

'I'm going to make Ben a shroud. We have proper customs here in England. It ain't fitting for a body just to be left.'

Suddenly the Doctor realised the reason for Reuben's hostility. 'You think *we* had something to do with Ben's death?'

'I know what I know. And what I think.'

'Incontrovertible,' said the Doctor politely.

Reuben glowered at him. 'Don't start talking in your own lingo neither, I won't have that.'

'What are you going to do? Clap us in irons?'

'I'm senior on this lighthouse now, and——'

'See here, I'm only trying to help you,' snapped the Doctor.

Reuben backed away. 'Vince and me'll manage. Now I'll just go and tend to poor Ben.'

'Stubborn old mule . . .' muttered the Doctor irritably.

Leela was still carrying the twisted remains of the lamp. 'You think the creature that did this will come back?'

'I just don't know.'

As always, Leela was in favour of direct action. 'If it is here on the rock we should take weapons and hunt it!'

The Doctor tapped the lamp with a long finger. 'I don't fancy playing tag in the darkness with something that can do this.' He paused for a moment. 'Young Vince is still pretty shaken. I think I'll go up and have a word with him. You stay here.'

The Doctor went out. As soon as he was gone, Leela slipped a heavy sailor's knife from her boot. She'd found it at the bottom of Vince's chest and appropriated it immediately. Despite the Doctor's prohibitions, Leela never felt properly dressed without a weapon. She hefted the knife thoughtfully, tested point and edge with her thumb, then set off down the stairs.

In the lamp room Reuben sat cross-legged by Ben's body, sewing the corpse into its shroud. Like all old sailors he was handy with needle and thread. He didn't hear Leela as she slipped silently past him and out into the fog.

*

The Doctor leaned against the lamp-room wall. Vince tended the steadily flashing light and gave regular blasts on the foghorn, while he told the Doctor about the light in the sky. The Doctor listened keenly. 'And what time was all this?'

'Couple of hours ago, just getting dark. It went down into the sea, over there.'

'How far away?'

'About a mile or two, near as I could tell. Dunno how big it was, you see. Soon after that the fog started to come down, and it got cold, all of a sudden like.'

'Yes,' said the Doctor thoughtfully. 'I noticed the cold. Good lad, Vince, you've been very observant.'

'Thank you, sir.' Vince was both flattered and puzzled by the Doctor's interest in his story.

The Doctor stared out at the fog that surrounded the tower. 'A fireball, eh? That might explain a great deal . . .'

Knife in hand, body poised for instant attack, Leela crept silently through the darkness. She had already covered most of the tiny island, and so far she had found nothing. She had hoped for some kind of tracks, but nothing showed on the bare rocky surface.

Her foot slipped and she almost tumbled into a shallow rock pool. She drew back, then paused, looking harder at the water. Something was floating on the surface of the pool. Several somethings, in fact. Leela knelt down. Fish! Tiny, dead fish.

There was a faint crackling behind her and she whirled round. She crouched motionless, listening, peering into the fog. But she saw nothing. Just the swirling fog. Stealthily she crept on, moving in the direction of the sound . . .

The Doctor was entertaining Vince with accounts of famous lighthouses he had visited during his travels. 'Of course, on Pharos they had terrible trouble keeping the bonfire alight. Mind you, they had plenty of slaves to carry wood . . .'

Vince nodded vaguely. 'I suppose it's all done different abroad. Didn't know they still had slaves though.'

(Vince didn't realise that the Doctor's visit to the famous Alexandrian lighthouse had taken place in the third century BC.)

Reuben entered and gave the Doctor a suspicious stare. He nodded to Vince. 'I'll take over here, lad. Time you got some supper.'

'I'm all right,' protested Vince. Somehow he found the Doctor's company reassuring.

'I'll take over,' insisted Reuben. 'Long night ahead of us.' He glared meaningfully at the Doctor. 'I expect you'll be tired, mister? There's bunks in the crew room.'

'Tired?' said the Doctor in surprise. 'No, no, not

a bit of it. You carry on, don't mind me.'

Reuben grunted. 'I've stoked the boiler, Vince, and made poor Ben decent.'

Vince nodded silently. He didn't like to think about the corpse down in the generator room.

Reuben glared at the Doctor, who gave him a cheerful smile. He turned back to Vince. 'Well, off you go, lad!'

Vince went.

Reuben gave the Doctor another dirty look, and this time the Doctor replied with a friendly wink.

Reuben turned away in disgust, reaching for his oil-can. Some people just didn't know when they weren't wanted.

Vince was on the landing by the crew room when he heard a dragging sound from down below. He paused, listening. The sound came again, like someone dragging a heavy sack. 'Is someone down there?' he called. There was no answer. Vince bit his lip. 'Ben?' he called fearfully. Still no answer. Just the dragging sound, moving away. Fearfully Vince began to descend the gloomy stairs. The light of his lantern cast wavering shadows on the walls.

Leela stood tensely in the darkness, feeling both frustrated and angry. She'd been close on the track of the crackling sound, then suddenly she had lost it, somewhere near the lighthouse. Now she was waiting, alert for the faintest sound.

Suddenly the crackling began again. It came nearer, nearer—and now it was mixed with a dragging sound . . .

Leela peered into the darkness. Was there a faint glow there beyond the densely swirling fog?

The crackling moved away. It became fainter, and then suddenly stopped. The creature had gone back into the sea, Leela decided. She headed back towards the lighthouse.

Fearfully, Vince crept into the generator room. It was brightly lit—and empty. The generator was throbbing steadily. Reluctantly he looked at the dark shape by the wall. With sudden horror he realised that the shape wasn't Ben's body after all. It was the ripped-open empty shroud. He ran to the speaking-tube and blew frantically. 'Reuben!' he screamed. 'Reuben, are you there? It's Ben! He's walking . . .'

In the lamp room Reuben took the speaker away from his ear and stared at it unbelievingly. 'What's that?' he bellowed. 'Talk sense, boy! Pull yourself together.'

Clutching the speaking-tube Vince babbled, 'It's true

I tell you. He's not down here now. He's gone! You said he'd walk. You said——' The outer door burst open with a crash. Vince gave a yell of fear and dropped the speaking-tube.

Leela stood in the doorway. 'Did you see it?' she demanded. 'Did it come here?'

Vince was too terrified to speak.

Reuben blew into the speaking-tube and yelled. 'Vince! What's going on down there?'

The Doctor had been on the outer gallery, staring out into the fog. Now he reappeared, tapping Reuben on the shoulder. 'There's a light out there!'

Confused and angry, the old man whirled round. 'What? What's that?'

'There's a light. Out there at sea. I think it's a ship.'

Leela had managed to shake his story out of Vince. She looked at him disbelievingly. 'The dead do not walk. It is impossible.'

'I heard this dragging noise, I tell you—and when I got down here he'd gone.'

'There was something out there on the rocks just now,' said Leela slowly. 'And I too heard a dragging sound . . .'

The speaking-tube gave a shrill blast. Automatically Vince picked it up and listened. 'It's Reuben. He says there's a ship just off the rocks. He says she's going to strike!'

The call to duty overcame Vince's fears and he began dashing up the stairs. With a baffled glance at the empty shroud Leela followed.

In the lamp room, everyone was round the great telescope. Reuben was at the eyepiece. 'It's a ship right enough. Steam yacht by the look of her.'

The Doctor took his place. Through the powerful telescope he could see the fog-shrouded shape of the ship, lights blazing as it ploughed recklessly through the waves, heading straight towards them. 'She's going too fast!'

'Fool to be going at all on a night like this,' said Reuben. 'Any skipper worth his ticket——'

The lamp went out.

Luckily the oil lamps were still burning. Reuben was taking no more chances with electricity. He ran to the siren and began sounding it frantically, sending bellow after bellow through the fog. 'Warning devices, Vince,' he shouted.

'I'll get 'em, Reuben.' Vince had already run down the steps to the service room. A moment later he reappeared, his arms full of rockets and maroons.

'Miss, you take over the siren,' shouted Reuben. He grabbed a Verey pistol and loaded it. The Doctor was already mounting a signal rocket on its firing stand.

'They'll strike any minute now,' shouted Reuben. He fired the Verey pistol and a red flare went sizzling out into the fog.

The ship was very close now and they could see frantic figures scurrying about on deck. Reuben was watching in fascinated horror. The Doctor lugged the signal rocket to the gallery rail, but Reuben waved him aside. 'It's no use, they're too late to alter course. She's going to strike!'

With a grinding crash the yacht smashed on to the jagged rocks.

4

The Survivors

'Too late, she's struck!' shouted Reuben. They caught a brief glimpse of the yacht through a break in the fog. She was well aground on the rocks, her bows thrust unnaturally high into the air. Then the fog closed in, hiding the wreck.

'What will happen now?' asked Leela.

'Sea'll pound her on those rocks till she breaks up, Miss.'

'Then they will all die.'

Leela's prosaic words reminded Reuben of his duty. 'If there are survivors we'll find 'em by East Crag. Tide'll bring 'em in. Mister, you keep that siren going. Vince, bring the rocket-line.'

The Doctor had no intention of missing all the excitement. 'Keep that siren going, Leela,' he ordered and rushed out after Reuben and Vince.

Leela went to the siren and pulled the lever. The deep booming note rang out, like the cry of a love-sick sea monster. Pleased with the effect, Leela pulled the lever again.

*

Reuben, Vince and the Doctor gathered rescue equipment from the service room, then hurried down the stairs. As they ran through the generator room, Reuben pointed to a coil of rope in the corner. 'Bring that rope, mister,' he ordered.

The Doctor went to obey, amused at the way in which the crisis had restored the old man's confidence. As he bent to pick up the rope, his hand brushed the metal guard-rail around the generator. There was a crackling sound and a flash of blue sparks. The Doctor snatched his hand away. The rail had given him a distinct electric shock.

Puzzled, the Doctor peered at the rail. It was quite separate from the generator. There was no reason for it to be live . . .

'You coming with that rope, mister?' shouted Reuben.

The Doctor threw the coil of rope over his shoulder and hurried off after the others.

Reuben led them through the foggy darkness at a run, to a point where a narrow cove cut into the coastline. They clambered down a rocky path on to a little shingle beach, and stared out to sea. 'Tide'll bring 'em here, if they got any boats away,' said Reuben confidently. He re-loaded the Verey pistol and fired, sending a red flare out into the fog. 'Ahoy there,' he called. 'Ahoy!'

Leela gave another blast on the foghorn, then wandered on to the outer gallery, feeling rather indignant the Doctor had managed to trick her into staying out of danger. She leaned over the rail, hoping to be able to see the rescue party. The fog cleared for a few moments and she suddenly caught a brief glimpse of a shapeless glowing mass, moving towards the sea. It slithered across an edge of rock and disappeared.

Leela stared in astonishment—and the lighthouse lamp came on.

Gazing round the little beach, Vince turned and saw the light. 'Reuben, the light is on again,' he called.

Reuben glanced briefly over his shoulder. 'Danged electricity, wouldn't happen with oil.'

'No, I don't think it would,' said the Doctor, almost to himself. 'It seems to need electricity.'

'Listen,' said Reuben, 'I think I heard something.' He fired off another Verey light and shouted again. 'Ahoy, there!'

'Ahoy . . .' A faint answering hail came drifting through the fog.

'This way,' bellowed Reuben, in a voice as loud as the foghorn itself. He fired off another Verey light. 'Vince, and you, mister, stand by with those lines.'

They waited tensely, staring out into the fog, while waves crashed on to the tiny beach. Then a shape loomed out of the darkness. It was a ship's lifeboat.

Reuben took the line from the Doctor, uncoiled it

and threw with surprising force. The line snaked out and a burly figure in the bows of the lifeboat caught it and made it fast. 'Come on now, haul,' ordered Reuben, and all three men began heaving on the line.

As soon as the lifeboat grated on the shingle, the seaman in the bows jumped out and helped them to haul it in. But before they could bring it much closer to land a second, smaller man took a flying leap from the boat, landing face down in the water.

The Doctor helped the spluttering figure to his feet, passed him along to Vince and turned to the other survivors. There were only two more of them, a tall military-looking man, and a shivering fair-haired girl. He helped them out of the boat and up on to the beach.

Not without difficulty Vince helped the soaking, bedraggled figure of the man who'd jumped, into the crew room. Reuben followed with the tall soldierly-looking man and the girl.

Vince's survivor collapsed gasping on a chair.

He was a stoutly-built man with a spoiled, self-indulgent look about him. Diamonds glinted from his cuff-links and tie-pin, and the rings on his plump fingers. His expensive-looking clothes were drenched with sea-water. Vince couldn't help feeling sorry for him.

He did his best to cheer the man up. 'You'll be

all right, sir. Come over by the stove and dry your-self.'

'Needn't have got so wet in the first place,' grumbled Reuben. 'No call to go jumping out like that.'

The soldierly man chuckled. 'His lordship was anxious to get ashore!'

'Brandy!' croaked the stout man faintly. 'Give me brandy.'

'Never you mind him and his brandy,' ordered Reuben. 'See to the young lady first.'

Obediently, Vince transferred his attentions to the shivering girl. 'Here ma'am, let me help you.' He lowered her into a chair and wrapped a blanket round her shoulders.

'I'm all right,' she whispered faintly.

'Well, I ain't,' said the stout man. 'I'm soaked to the skin.'

'Sea water's healthy, Henry,' mocked the tall man.

The other gave him a filthy look. 'I need a drink, I tell you. I'll catch my death like this.' He caught Vince by the sleeve. 'Get me a brandy, young fellow.'

Vince pulled away and began tipping coal on the iron stove. 'You don't need no brandy, sir,' he said cheerily. 'Hot soup's the ticket for you. I'll get you all some in a minute.'

'Don't tell me what I need,' said the other peevishly. 'Dammit, hasn't anybody got a flask?'

Reuben looked disgustedly at him. 'You see to 'em as best you can, Vince. I'd better go up and check on the lamp.'

Vince poked the coals into a blaze and then turned to the girl. 'Come over to the stove and get yourself warm, miss.'

He moved her chair closer to the stove and she hunched over it, warming her hands. 'Thank you, that's very kind of you. What's your name?'

'Vince, miss. Vince Hawkins.'

'Thank you, Hawkins,' said the young lady graciously.

Vince stammered, 'I'd best get on with that soup . . .' He hurried off to the kitchen. The stout man glared indignantly after him, and the tall man smiled in sardonic amusement, enjoying the other's discomfiture.

On the lamp-room gallery, the Doctor and Leela were talking in low voices. Leela told the Doctor about the glowing shape she had seen on the rocks.

'What was it like?' asked the Doctor.

'I couldn't see it clearly. But it shone, like a rotten fungus in the forest.'

'Luminous . . . Do you think you could take me to the place where you saw it?'

'Yes, I think so.'

'Good. Don't tell the others. We don't want a panic.'

'What do you think be going on here, mister?' asked a voice behind them. Reuben was standing by the door.

46

'I don't know,' said the Doctor frankly. 'When I find out, I'll tell you.'

'Wouldn't try to find out too much. Some things it ain't wise to meddle with . . .'

'What do you mean, old one?' asked Leela.

'I reckon I know what you saw. They always said the Beast of Fang Rock would come back.'

'The Beast of Fang Rock?'

'Aye,' said Reuben. And with gloomy relish, he launched into a long rambling tale of tragedy in the early days of the lighthouse. A three-man crew had been overtaken by some mysterious and tragic fate. 'When the relief boat come, there was only one left alive, and he was stark staring mad. They found the body of the second cold and dead in the lamp room —and the third was found floating in the sea. Two dead, one mad—that was the work of the Beast! And now it's back.'

In the crew room Vince was still fussing round the blonde young lady. The tall man looked on with quiet amusement, the stout one kept up a constant stream of protest. 'I need some dry clothes, and I need them now,' he said petulantly.

'All in good time, sir! I'll just give the young lady her soup, and then I'll get round to you.'

'But I'll catch my death of cold standing about like this!'

'Shouldn't be so impulsive, Henry,' said the tall

man with mock concern. 'Jumping right out of the boat like that!'

'When I want your opinion, I'll ask for it. Now, what about this brandy, young fellow? Surely you keep some in the medical supplies?'

Vince shook his head. 'No liquor allowed on this lighthouse, sir. Against regulations.'

The stout man said angrily, 'To hell with your regulations——' He broke off as the Doctor and Leela came into the room.

The Doctor looked round. 'Where's the other man, your cox'n?'

'Oh, Harker, he stayed to secure the boat, I believe. No doubt he'll be up directly.'

'Good. I'll wait.' The Doctor sat down, and there was a moment of uneasy silence. Leela stood in the doorway, looking round the little group. She could feel the tension in the air.

'Excellent fellow, Harker,' drawled the tall man. 'It was his seamanship got us ashore.'

'Whose seamanship was it that got you on the rocks in the first place?' asked the Doctor blandly.

The tall man looked sharply at him. 'I don't believe we've met, sir. Are you in charge here?'

'No—but I'm full of ideas.'

Vince brought bowls of soup for the two men and said, 'Beg pardon, Doctor, but I think it's time I stoked the boilers.' He looked appealingly at the Doctor, making no attempt to move.

'Off you go then, Vince. Leela, you go with him.'

Vince and Leela left, and the girl looked reprovingly at the Doctor. 'You're a Doctor then?'

'That's right.'

'And you send a woman to stoke boilers?' The young lady was obviously shocked.

'Leela's a rather unusual young lady. Besides, one of the keepers was electrocuted this evening. Since then young Vince doesn't like to go to the generator room alone.'

The soldierly man nodded understandingly. 'Disturbing thing for a young fellow, the first sight of death. Remember when I was in India . . .'

The other man groaned. 'Oh not one of your army stories, Jimmy. They're even more boring than your House of Commons anecdotes.'

The Doctor looked curiously at the two men. They were travelling companions, and presumably friends, yet they were completely different types, one laconic and soldierly, the other like a spoiled, greedy child. Moreover, they spoke to each other as if they were bitter enemies. He decided that it would help if he had names to attach to all these new faces. He addressed the tall man. 'Shouldn't we introduce ourselves?'

'Yes, of course. The young lady is Miss Adelaide Lesage, Lord Palmerdale's confidential secretary. The wet gentleman is Lord Henry Palmerdale, the well-known financier. And I'm Colonel James Skinsale, Member of Parliament for Thurley. And you are . . .?'

'I'm the Doctor—my companion's name is Leela. Where were you heading for, when your yacht struck?'

It was Lord Palmerdale who answered. 'Southampton. I've a special train waiting to take me to London. I must be there before the Stock Exchange opens.'

Adelaide sighed theatrically. 'The pressures of business, you know. If we'd been able to stay on in Deauville none of this would have happened.'

'We'd popped across the Channel in the yacht,' explained Palmerdale airily. 'We all had a little flutter in the Casino. Though in Jimmy's case it was more of a plunger—eh Jimmy?'

'You're very cheerful for a man whose yacht has been wrecked,' Skinsale said sourly.

Palmerdale waved a disparaging hand. 'Insured.'

'What about the crew?' asked the Doctor. 'Were any other boats launched?'

Skinsale shrugged. 'I'm afraid we didn't wait to see, Doctor. His Lordship was in rather a hurry to leave the sinking ship!'

Palmerdale shot him a venomous look. 'I've already told you, it's imperative that I reach London before the stock market opens.'

'Oh, was that the reason?' drawled Skinsale.

'I'm afraid you've no chance of getting to London tonight,' said the Doctor firmly. 'Not in this fog.'

Skinsale gave a sudden bark of laughter. 'The wheel of fortune, eh, Henry? Perhaps you didn't win all you thought at the Casino.'

Leela kept watch while Vince shovelled coal into the boiler. As he flung on the last shovel of coal she said, 'Listen!'

'What? I can't hear nothing . . .'

'Something is *dragging* over the rocks towards us!'

'Ben?' whispered Vince fearfully. 'He be coming back. Coming back for me!'

Leela grabbed him by the shoulders and shook him. 'Go and tell the Doctor. Call him from the room before you tell him, and don't let the others hear. Give me that!'

Leela took the shovel from Vince's hands and gave him a push. As he fled, she took up her position behind the outer door, shovel raised like an axe.

The dragging sound was very near now. Slowly the door started to open . . .

5

Return of the Dead

The door creaked slowly open and a massive shape appeared in the doorway. It backed into the room, dragging a heavy burden, wrapped up in an old tarpaulin.

Leela put the cold metal of the shovel against its neck. 'Don't move!'

The figure swung round, revealing itself to be a massive barrel-chested man in a blue seaman's jersey. Leela backed away, shovel raised to strike. 'I said don't move!'

'It's all right, Leela,' said the Doctor's voice behind her. 'This one's a friend—aren't you Harker?'

The big seaman gave a puzzled nod. 'That's right, sir. I was delayed, d'ye see. I found this.' He pulled back the tarpaulin.

The Doctor looked at the mangled shape at Harker's feet. 'Poor wretch.'

Leela came forward. 'What is it, Doctor?'

'All that's left of poor Ben, I'm afraid. Where did you find him, Harker?'

'In the sea, sir. Came drifting in when I moored the boat.' He looked down at the body, then looked hurriedly away. 'Terrible what the sea can do to a man . . .'

'It wasn't the sea that did that.' The Doctor paused. 'Harker, there's hot soup waiting in the crew room. It's just up those stairs. The others are already there.'

'Aye, aye, sir,' said Harker obediently, and went off.

The Doctor pulled the body away from the door and closed it. He covered it over again with the tarpaulin.

Leela was no stranger to violent death, but even she was glad to see the body covered up. 'Do you think the Beast attacked him, Doctor?'

'What Beast?'

'The Beast of Fang Rock.'

'No such animal—not in the way Reuben means.'

'Reuben said there was.'

'Leela, the people who live in these parts have been fisher folk for generations. They're almost as primitive and superstition-riddled as your lot!'

Leela wasn't convinced. 'Reuben's story about those men . . . Two dead, one mad.'

'One man kills the other in a brawl, jumps in the sea in a fit of remorse. Third man spends weeks with a corpse for company and goes out of his mind.'

'All right, then, what about this body? What about those—marks?'

'Post mortem,' said the Doctor briefly. 'Something wanted to make a detailed study of human anatomy. That's why it took Ben's body.'

Vince's voice came down the stairs. 'Doctor? Are you there?'

'Quick,' said the Doctor. They wrapped the body securely in its tarpaulin and thrust it into a corner. Vince came in and looked apprehensively at Leela. 'That noise . . . Did you find out what it was?'

'It was only the seaman, returning from the boat,' said the Doctor.

'But the dragging sound?'

Before the Doctor could stop her Leela said, 'He was bringing back Ben's body. He found it floating in the sea.'

Vince gasped. 'So he did walk! It's true what Reuben said . . .'

'Stop that, Vince,' said Leela sharply. 'I have told you, the dead don't walk.'

Vince gave the Doctor an agonised look. 'But you said he was dead. How did he get in the sea?'

The Doctor made his voice calm and reassuring. 'Obviously I was too hasty, Vince. Massive electric shock can produce a death-like coma. Poor Ben recovered consciousness, staggered out on to the rocks, fell into the sea and was finally drowned.' Vince stared at him unbelievingly. 'Time you got on with your work,' said the Doctor briskly. 'There's nothing supernatural happening—just a tragic accident.'

'He wasn't breathing when *I* saw him, that I'll swear.'

'I told you, he was in a coma. Electricity has strange effects, you know.'

54

Vince nodded slowly. 'Yes, I suppose it must have been the electricity. Sorry, Doctor, I reckon I made a bit of a fool of myself.'

He turned and went slowly away.

When he was out of earshot, Leela whispered, 'Why didn't you tell him the truth?'

The Doctor stared broodingly at the tarpaulin-covered body. 'Because I don't know what the truth is—yet!'

Harker sat silently by the stove, his big hands clasped round a steaming mug of soup. 'You moored the boat securely?' demanded Palmerdale.

Harker looked up at him and nodded, but didn't speak.

'Good. When you're rested we'll make for the mainland.'

Skinsale said, 'Are you mad, Henry?'

'I've made up my mind. It's the only way.'

'But it's out of the question. Good Lord, in a fog like this . . .'

'It can't be more than five or six miles,' said Palmerdale impatiently. 'No trouble at all to a sea-man like Harker here.'

Skinsale threw up his hands in despair and turned to the girl. 'Reason with him, Adelaide. Perhaps you can make him see sense.'

Before Adelaide could speak Palmerdale shouted, 'You two can come with me, or you can stay here, just as you wish. My mind is made up.'

Harker slammed his mug down on the table. 'And so's mine. I'm not taking a boat out in this.'

Palmerdale stared at him as though a chair or a table had suddenly found a voice. He took it for granted that the lower orders did as they were told. '*What* did you say, Harker?'

'I'll take no boat out, not after what I've seen tonight. And that's flat.'

'Damn your insolence,' spluttered Palmerdale. 'You're my employee, and you'll obey my order.'

'Will I?' Harker turned away and spat into the stove.

Skinsale chuckled. 'Hang him from the yard arm, Henry. This is mutiny!'

Abandoning Harker for the moment, Palmerdale turned to a different grievance. 'As I see it, the accident was entirely due to inefficiency on the part of the lighthouse service. So they have the responsibility of seeing I reach the mainland.'

'That won't wash, old chap,' said Skinsale scornfully. 'You can't possibly expect the lighthouse people——'

Adelaide joined in to support her employer. 'His lordship is quite right,' she said primly. 'If the light had been working . . .'

'We'd still have struck the rocks, at the speed we were going,' said Skinsale.

Harker looked up from the fire. 'You're right

there, sir. We should have been going dead slow in them conditions. And it weren't the Captain's fault, neither.'

Palmerdale went red with anger. 'That's quite enough, Harker. The fact remains that the light wasn't working. There'll be an inquiry, I assure you.'

'The inquiry has already begun,' said another voice. The Doctor was in the doorway, Leela beside him.

Skinsale gaped at him. 'What inquiry? What are you talking about?'

'I just thought I ought to come up and warn you. Keep together, and stay here, in this room. Harker, you ought to get some rest.'

Harker rose obediently, went over to a bunk and stretched out, pulling a blanket over him. The Doctor and Leela went back downstairs, leaving the rest of the castaways gaping after them.

'Amazing air of authority, that chap,' said Skinsale thoughtfully. 'I wonder who he really is?'

Palmerdale slumped into a chair. 'If you ask me, the fellow's not quite all there.' He tapped his forehead meaningfully. 'Those staring eyes . . . always a bad sign, that! Girl's probably his nurse.'

Adelaide pursed her lips. 'There's certainly something very strange about her.'

Skinsale grinned. 'Dunno about strange . . . but she ain't a bad looker.'

'Positively uncivilised in my view. Perhaps you

spent too long in India, Colonel Skinsale!'

'Long enough to learn to appreciate the beauties of nature, my dear.'

Adelaide sniffed disdainfully. 'Since we seem compelled to spend the night in this frightful place, do you think there is a private bedroom where I might get some sleep?'

Skinsale nodded towards the speaking-tube on the wall. 'Well, if this contraption works, I'll see what the proprietors of the establishment have to say.' He picked up the speaking-tube and blew.

The tube whistled shrilly in the lamp room, and Reuben picked it up. 'Ahoy there, what is it?' He listened then said impatiently, 'There's Ben's room, she be welcome to that. He won't be needing it no more.' He hung up the tube. 'Trouble with the gentry, they always wants running after.'

Vince had gone out on to the gallery, and was looking down. 'Reuben, there's someone out there. See them lights?'

Reuben came out on to the gallery. He could just make out the glow of a lantern bobbing about on the rocks. 'It's the Doctor and that girl.'

'They've no cause to be out there,' said Vince uneasily.

Reuben grunted. 'Well, they can't say I didn't warn them. I warned 'em both, right here on this very spot.'

'Warned 'em? What about?'

'The Beast of Fang Rock,' said Reuben solemnly.

Vince gave an uneasy laugh. 'You still on about that old tale?'

'More than a tale, lad. The girl *saw* it tonight. All glowing, like they said . . .'

'She couldn't have seen it . . .'

Reuben lowered his voice. 'Last time the Beast was seen on Fang Rock was eighty year ago. Two men died that night . . .'

Fog swirled dankly round the sea-wet rocks, and the lantern cast only a tiny circle of yellow light.

Leela took a bearing on the nearby lighthouse. 'I'm sure it was somewhere near here I saw it. Close to that flat-topped rock.'

The Doctor fished a compass from his pocket and set it on the rock. The needle spun crazily. 'Aha!' said the Doctor in satisfaction.

Leela looked at the spinning compass needle. 'And what does that tell you?'

'It has a very strong electrical field, strong enough to kill a man on contact . . .' The Doctor picked up the compass and moved on. He seemed to be following some kind of trail. It led him to the pool where Leela had found the dead fish. They were still there, floating on the surface of the pool. 'Or kill fish at a distance of several yards,' concluded the Doctor.

'And what do you think it is?'

The Doctor looked round. The fog was closing in and the lighthouse suddenly seemed very far away. 'I don't know what it is—but I think it's desperate, and I think it's cunning and I think we'd better be getting back!'

As they headed back towards the lighthouse, the faintest of crackling sounds came from behind a nearby rock. A glowing shape slid out from its hiding place and flowed across the rocks.

6

Attack from the Unknown

When Skinsale came back into the crew room, Harker was sleeping soundly, Palmerdale slumped disconsolately in his chair.

'I think Adelaide will sleep now,' said Skinsale cheerfully.

Palmerdale looked up sardonically. 'Oh, splendid. That's the main thing, isn't it—that my secretary gets a good night's sleep.'

'You'd do well to get some yourself,' said Skinsale amiably. He stretched out on a bunk.

'Sleep? Here, in this hovel?'

Skinsale looked round the crew room. 'Quite a snug little bivouac, this. I've slept in worst places when I was in the Army.'

'Ah, but that was before you retired and went into politics,' sneered Palmerdale. 'Got a taste for good living then, didn't you?'

Palmerdale's rudeness only seemed to increase the other man's good humour. 'Feeling a little frustrated, old chap?'

'Why the hell shouldn't I, when I've been cheated like this?' exploded Palmerdale.

Skinsale's voice hardened. 'I think you'd better watch your tongue. I kept my part of the bargain. I gave you secret advance information about the Government's financial plans. I was a fool and a knave, but I did it. You tore up my gambling IOUs —now we're even!'

'What *use* is your blasted information if I can do nothing with it?'

'Quite. Amusing, isn't it?' Skinsale yawned luxuriously.

'I could still expose you,' threatened Palmerdale.

'Do be reasonable, old chap. If the information is never used, where's the proof I ever gave it? And you're forgetting something else.'

'Am I? What, pray?'

'I'm an officer and a gentleman, Henry. You're a nobody, a jumped-up little moneygrubber for all your bought title. Besmirch my good name and I'll sue you for every penny you've got! So, good night to you.'

Colonel Skinsale closed his eyes and went peacefully to sleep.

The Doctor and Leela came into the generator room. Nothing had changed. The tarpaulin-wrapped body still lay in its corner, the generator was still throbbing away.

Leela looked out into the foggy darkness behind

62

them, and then closed the door. 'You think this creature will return?'

The Doctor nodded. 'I think it was taking Ben's body away for examination when you saw it from the gallery.'

'Into the sea?'

'*Under* the sea . . . Earlier tonight Vince saw something he called a fireball. It fell into the sea not far away.'

'Another TARDIS?'

'Not a TARDIS—but very possibly some kind of space-craft. An alien, a creature who had never encountered human beings before, might well behave in just this way.'

'Why would it come here? There is nothing on this foggy rock.'

The Doctor pointed to the generator. 'There's power—electricity. Perhaps that attracted it.'

'An alien creature travelling through space—and you said it was desperate, Doctor?'

'Its behaviour pattern is—furtive. It keeps out of sight, spies out the land, weighs up its chances of a successful attack.'

'Then we are not facing a bold enemy?'

'Not bold but cunning, Leela. This fog is no freak of the weather. It was deliberately contrived to isolate us. Now the creature is growing more confident. It's seen this primitive technology, studied the physical limitations of its enemies.' The Doctor sighed, and said gloomily, 'All in all, I've a feeling we're in a lot of trouble!'

'Do not be afraid, Doctor. We shall arm ourselves and post guards. The others will help.'

'We'll have to convince them of the danger first. If we start talking about creatures from space, they'll just think we're mad.'

'We shall explain that we come from space ourselves,' said Leela triumphantly. 'We are not of this Earth, or of this time.'

The Doctor shuddered. 'Don't tell them that, whatever you do.' He remembered something Leela had said a few moments earlier. 'What do you mean, afraid?'

Lord Palmerdale stood looking thoughtfully down at the telegraph. By now Skinsale was fast asleep. Palmerdale crept over to Harker and shook him roughly by the shoulder. 'Wake up, man,' he whispered. 'Wake up!'

Harker awoke in sudden panic, like a man in the middle of a nightmare. 'Look out, look out,' he muttered. 'She's going to strike.'

Palmerdale shook him again. 'That's all over and done with. Wake up, will you?'

Still half-asleep, Harker stared dazedly at him. 'What is it? What d'you want?'

'Do you know how to use a Morse apparatus?'

'Do I what?'

'Can you use a Morse telegraph apparatus, like the one over there?'

'Course I can!'

'Splendid! I want you to send a message for me. It's to be passed on to my brokers in London.'

Sleepily Harker rubbed a hand across his eyes. 'Send a message to London? What about?'

'It's merely an instruction to sell certain shares and buy others. Nothing that need concern you. Just do as I tell you. It's a very important business matter and there's a great deal of money involved.'

'Money?'

'Don't worry, you'll be handsomely rewarded. I had urgent reasons for getting back to London, but this will do just as well.'

'I remember you was mad to get back to England,' said Harker slowly. 'I remember on the bridge, when the fog was coming down. Captain begging for permission to slow down, you telling him full speed ahead and damn the fog.'

'I was the owner,' said Palmerdale angrily. 'It was his duty to obey my orders!'

'He was old and weak, scared he'd never get another ship. You made him do it!'

'Never mind all that, Harker. Just do as I tell you and you'll be well paid.'

Harker rose slowly to his feet, his massive bulk towering over his employer. 'Then, when the ship struck, it was get the owner away, and the owner's fancy woman and the owner's fine friend. Never mind the poor sailor, he can take his chances.'

'I'll have no more of your insolence, Harker. I've offered to pay you . . .'

Harker grabbed Palmerdale by the collar and lifted him off his feet. 'Pay?' he roared. 'There's good mates of mine feeding the fishes because of you. Will you pay for that?'

He tightened his grip on Palmerdale's collar, shaking him to and fro.

'No,' choked Palmerdale. 'No! Get him off!'

Roused by the noise, Skinsale woke up, realised what was happening and tried to pull Harker away. The big seaman flung him aside, and went on throttling Palmerdale.

The Doctor and Leela arrived just in time. The Doctor flung himself on Harker, and Leela and Skinsale came to help. It took *all* their efforts to pull Harker from his victim.

'Harker, that's enough,' shouted the Doctor. 'Do you want to kill him?'

Harker flung Palmerdale aside, and he dropped choking on to a bunk. Harker glowered down at him. 'There's good seamen dead because of him. He deserves to die.'

'We've got our own lives to worry about now,' said the Doctor grimly. 'I've got news for you, gentlemen. This lighthouse is under attack. Before morning we could all be dead. Is anyone interested?'

*

It came out of the sea, and slid over the edge of the rocks on to the island. Its many-faceted eyes saw the lighthouse, with its flashing light. It had studied its enemies and made its plans. Now it was time to act. Swiftly and silently the glowing shape moved towards the lighthouse.

'Time that boiler was stoked, boy,' said Reuben gruffly.

Vince nodded, but he didn't move. 'Reuben, you don't really believe what happened all those years ago is happening again? The Beast and all that?'

'There's three of us, and there were three of them. Two dead, one mad. Ben's dead, isn't he? And the night's not over yet.'

Vince stood there white and trembling, and Reuben said, 'You're shaking too much to hold a shovel, boy. Stay here, I'll do the boiler.'

'Well if you're sure,' said Vince eagerly. He tried to pull himself together. 'I'll go if you like . . .'

Reuben shook his head and stumped off.

The Doctor was finishing his speech of warning. The problem was to impress his audience without giving them any real facts. 'No one, no one at all must go outside the lighthouse, for any reason,' he concluded. 'Is that clear?'

Palmerdale had recovered his breath, and his self-assurance. 'No, it's not clear. Lot of ridiculous mumbo-jumbo if you ask me. Just what is this mysterious threat that's supposed to be lurking outside?'

Reuben came on to the landing in time to hear Palmerdale's question. He paused in the doorway and looked at the Doctor. 'You've told 'em you've seen it, have you? Told 'em the Beast is back.'

Skinsale gave an incredulous laugh. 'What Beast?'

'There's always death on the rock when the Beast's about.'

'Preposterous rubbish,' exploded Palmerdale. 'What is the old fool saying?'

Reuben glared malevolently at him. 'I'm saying that what's happened before will happen again.' He disappeared down the stairs.

The Doctor sighed. Reuben's intervention had come at just the wrong time, reducing his warnings of danger to an old wives' tale they could all laugh at.

'Superstitious old idiot,' said Palmerdale dismissively. 'If you expect us to take notice of some drunken fisherman's tale, Doctor . . .'

Leela decided to apply her own brand of persuasion. She whipped the knife from her boot and thrust it dangerously close to Palmerdale's chest. 'Silence, fat one. You will do as the Doctor instructs, or I will cut out your heart.'

Palmerdale was too terrified to speak.

The Doctor smiled. Perhaps there was something to be said for Leela's methods of persuasion. 'You heard what she said, old chap. And I warn you, she means it—don't you Leela?'

Leela didn't reply. She was staring into space, her whole body tense.

'What is it, Leela?'

'It's getting cold again.'

'You're sure?'

'Yes. The last time it felt cold like this—like a cold wave.'

The Doctor concentrated, testing the atmosphere. 'Yes, I think you're right.'

'Well, I can't feel anything,' said Skinsale.

'Leela's senses are particularly acute,' said the Doctor. 'And if she says it's getting colder—it's getting colder.'

He turned at the sound of movement in the doorway. It was Adelaide. She was wrapped in a blanket, shivering and only half awake. 'What's going on? Something woke me up ... I suddenly felt so cold ...'

'Nothing for you to worry about, Adelaide,' said Skinsale reassuringly.

The electric lights flickered.

They flickered down in the generator room too, where Reuben was stoking the boiler. He paused, looked suspiciously at a pressure gauge. Everything seemed normal. He flung on a few more shovels of coal, exhausting the little pile by the boiler door.

With a muttered curse he went over to the door of the coal store and flung it open.

Adelaide looked wildly round the room, wondering why everyone was acting so strangely. 'I don't understand what's wrong with you all. Please, Lord Palmerdale, what's happening?'

Skinsale glared warningly at Palmerdale, who cleared his throat and said, 'Nothing, my dear. There's absolutely nothing wrong . . .'

The electric lights went out, and a terrifying scream came echoing up the stairs.

7

The Enemy Within

Adelaide's own scream of terror merged with the piercing scream from below, and she flung herself into Skinsale's arms. The Doctor and Leela were already racing towards the sound.

At the door of the generator room, the Doctor held up a warning hand. He stepped cautiously inside. The darkly-shadowed room was empty. The door to the outside was standing ajar, and fog was seeping into the room. 'It's taken Reuben,' said the Doctor. 'It can't have got far—we may still be in time to save him. Come on, Leela—and don't step on any jellyfish!'

They ran out into the night.

Adelaide was on the verge of hysterics, and Skinsale and Palmerdale tried vainly to calm her down.

'That ghastly scream,' she sobbed. 'What was it? I know something terrible has happened.'

'Control yourself,' said Palmerdale irritably. He was frightened enough himself, and Adelaide was making things worse.

Skinsale patted her soothingly on the back. 'It's all right, my dear,' he said, 'there's no cause for alarm.'

Adelaide refused to be consoled. 'I knew I should never have come on this cruise. My astrologer Miss Nethercott warned me about danger by sea. It was in my stars!'

Skinsale produced a large white handkerchief and handed it to her. 'Come now, that's nonsense. You're overwrought . . .'

Adelaide sniffed into the handkerchief and her sobs began to subside.

Palmerdale saw that Harker had picked up an oil-lantern and was heading for the door. 'Harker! Where do you think you're going, man?'

'Below. Doctor may need help.' Harker shoved him aside and went on down the stairs.

'Insubordinate ruffian!' said Palmerdale indignantly. 'If there is something dangerous on this rock, we should all stick together!'

Skinsale gave one of his cynical grins. 'That's the ticket, Henry, surround yourself with people! With any luck the Beast will satisfy its appetite before it gets to you!'

This was too much for Adelaide. 'Stop it, stop it,' she screamed. 'Don't say such horrible things.' She collapsed in tears.

Palmerdale looked at Skinsale. 'Now see what you've done, you fool. You've set her off again!'

*

Harker came into the generator room. 'Doctor?' he called. 'Are you there?' He saw the outside door was still open. The Doctor and Leela must have gone outside. He crossed to the door and stood looking out into the swirling fog, but there was nothing to be seen.

For a moment Harker hesitated, wondering whether to follow the Doctor. Then he heard movement behind him and whirled round.

Reuben stood swaying in the doorway to the coal store, white-faced and glassy-eyed.

Harker stared at him. 'Reuben! Is something wrong, mate?'

Reuben's voice was thick, distorted, scarcely recognisable. 'Leave me be.' He staggered towards the stairs.

Harker looked worriedly after him, wishing desperately that the Doctor was back. He turned and shouted. 'Doctor, ahoy there . . .' His voice boomed out into the fog, but there was no reply.

Reuben climbed the stairs with agonising slowness, hauling himself up by the hand-rail. The wail of the foghorn came down from above and he paused, staring upwards with dead, inhuman eyes. He resumed his laborious climb.

Vince gave a final blast on the horn, and with startling suddenness the lamp came on again. Vince shook his head in perplexity. How long would the lights stay on this time? He had a nasty feeling the intervals were getting shorter . . .

Adelaide was still sobbing. Skinsale gave a sigh of relief as the electric lighting came on again. 'You see, they've repaired the lights again, my dear. It's all right, there's nothing to worry about now.'

Palmerdale was hovering nervously near the door. 'Listen!' he hissed. 'There's someone coming . . .'

He looked appealingly at Skinsale who moved quietly over to the door.

'Colonel, please, don't,' whispered Adelaide.

'Sssh!' whispered Palmerdale agitatedly. He wanted to know who was on the stairs, but he didn't want to be the one to go and find out.

Skinsale went on to the gloomy landing. 'Doctor, is that you? Harker?'

Dragging footsteps came up the stairs, and Reuben appeared. His face was deathly white, his eyes fixed and staring. Skinsale stared at him. 'Are you all right? Where are you off to?' Reuben shuffled past without a word.

Skinsale went back into the crew room. 'It's all right, it was only the old chap. He went straight on up the stairs. He looked pretty done in.' He turned to Adelaide. 'The crisis seems to be over, my dear. Why don't you go and lie down?'

Adelaide shuddered. 'Up there alone? Have you

taken leave of your senses, Colonel? I shall stay down here!'

Skinsale sighed.

At last there was an answer to Harker's repeated shouts. Suddenly, 'Harker! Is that you?' called a familiar voice.

He saw a lantern bobbing through the fog, and the Doctor and Leela appeared. 'We heard you calling,' said the Doctor. 'There's nothing out there now —nothing we could find, anyway.' They came into the room and the Doctor said, 'Let's get that door shut!' He slammed it behind them, and stood leaning against it, lost in thought. 'You know what I think?'

Leela looked puzzled. 'The creature has killed Reuben?'

'I'm afraid so,' said the Doctor. 'But that's not what I meant. I was wondering if I could work out its size . . .'

'Reuben's all right,' interrupted Harker. 'I've just seen him.'

The Doctor didn't seem to hear him. 'It would seem that every time it comes within a certain range of the generator . . .'

Leela turned to Harker. 'What did you say?'

'Reuben's all right,' he repeated. 'I just saw him go upstairs.'

The Doctor was lost in a maze of calculations. 'U,

by Q, over R,' he said mysteriously.

Leela tugged at his sleeve. 'Doctor, did you hear that?'

'Sssh, Savage,' said the Doctor reprovingly.

'What are you doing?'

'Thinking!' The Doctor touched the metal rail. There was a crackle of blue sparks. He snatched his hand away, sucking his fingers. 'Yes, it's certainly been here. You see, Harker, in the space which surrounds an electrically charged body an electrical potential occurs which is roughly proportional to the charge Q and inversely proportional to the distance R from the centre . . .' His voice tailed away as he became aware that Harker and Leela were staring at him with blank incomprehension. Suddenly the Doctor said sharply, 'Well, then, where is he?'

By now Harker was thoroughly confused. 'Who, sir?'

'Reuben. You said you'd seen him.'

'He went upstairs, sir. Looked like he'd seen a ghost.'

'Why didn't you *tell* me?'

'Well I tried, sir. I told the young lady here.'

'Why am I wasting my time trying to work out its size, eh? Why?'

Harker scratched his head. 'I'm sure I don't know, sir.'

'If Reuben's seen it, then obviously he can tell us!'

'That's what I thought,' said Leela. 'But then, I'm only a Savage!'

The Doctor grinned. 'Come on then, Savage, we'll go and find him. Harker, can you secure that door?'

'I reckon wedges'd do it best.'

'Then get on with it. I want us sealed in this lighthouse till morning.'

The Doctor and Leela hurried up the stairs.

Adelaide lay dozing on a bunk with a blanket over her. Skinsale too had stretched out again, but Palmerdale was on his feet pacing restlessly about the room. He paused in front of the telegraph set and stared longingly at it. Then he turned to Skinsale, his voice warm and friendly. 'I don't suppose you learned anything useful in the army, Jimmy? Like how to use one of these gadgets?'

'And you surely don't suppose I'd send a message to your brokers for you?'

'We could make a real killing, old boy,' said Palmerdale persuasively. 'Tell you what, not only will I forget your IOUs, I'll even split the profits with you. What could be fairer than that?'

Skinsale stared at him in astonishment. You could say one thing for Palmerdale, he was consistent. Even in the middle of the dangers that surrounded them, he still had his mind fixed firmly on making a profit. 'Look, Henry, if the word got out I'd given you that information, I'd be ruined, and you know it. Money isn't everything, you know!'

Palmerdale was still trying to grapple with this novel thought when the Doctor appeared in the doorway. 'Where is he?'

'Who?'

'Reuben.'

'Saw him on the stairs a few minutes ago,' said Skinsale.

'Doctor, what's happening?' demanded Palmerdale indignantly. 'I insist on an explanation.'

The Doctor ignored him. 'How did Reuben look?'

Skinsale considered. 'Groggy,' he said finally.

'Groggy?'

'Yes, Doctor. Decidedly groggy.'

Adelaide sat up. 'Doctor, what was that terrible cry we heard?'

The Doctor said, 'Thanks very much, Colonel. Come on, Leela.' They hurried off.'

Adelaide was indignant. 'Really! That man's manners are quite insufferable.'

'Things on his mind by the look of him,' said Skinsale thoughtfully. 'Eh, Henry?'

'We all have!' said Palmerdale shortly, and went abruptly out of the room.

Adelaide was still concerned with the social shortcomings of the Doctor and his companion. 'As for that girl, it's disgraceful the way she follows him about. You'd think she was tied to him by a piece of string . . .'

Skinsale stared after Palmerdale. 'Where would

you say his lordship's off to, Adelaide?'

'Is it important? None of us can go far on this dreadful place.'

'You know, some people make me nervous when I'm with 'em. Your employer has the opposite effect. I get nervous when he's out of my sight!' He made for the door.

'Colonel, you're not going to leave me here, alone?'

'Don't worry, my dear, back in a minute.'

Skinsale hurried out.

Adelaide rose to follow him, thought of the gloomy staircase and decided to stay where she was. She sat down again, huddling inside the blanket. Would morning never come? And why was it so cold . . .

The Doctor and Leela looked for Reuben in the lamp room, but Vince had seen no sign of him. He suggested the old man might be in Ben's room. They went back downstairs, and along a short corridor, which ended in a closed door. The Doctor hammered on it with his fist. 'Reuben! Reuben, can you hear me? Are you in there? Are you all right?'

There was no reply.

Reuben was standing quite motionless, staring at the window. The Doctor's voice could be heard quite clearly, but it produced no reaction.

Reuben went over to the window and flung it open. Cold air and fog flooded into the little room. Reuben's body seemed to blur and glow in the darkness . . .

8

The Bribe

The Doctor abandoned his banging and shouting and turned away.

Leela stared at the closed door. 'Why doesn't the old one answer?'

'He's not listening!'

'Not listening? Why not? We wish only to help him.'

'If he saw the creature and escaped from it, he'll have had a terrible shock—and shock can close the mind. He could stay like this for hours.'

'What shall we do?'

'For a start, somebody's got to keep the lighthouse running. You go down and tell Harker to keep the boiler-pressure up.'

'Keep the boiler-pressure up,' repeated Leela dutifully. She went back along the corridor and down the stairs chanting, 'Keep the boiler-pressure up. Keep the boiler-pressure up . . .'

'Lonely life you chaps lead here, eh?'

Vince jumped. Palmerdale was in the lamp-room

doorway, smiling affably.

Vince was always uneasy with the gentry, but he was glad of company, even Lord Palmerdale's. 'That it is, sir. Still you soon get used to it.'

Palmerdale came into the room. 'Don't suppose they pay you much either.'

'Oh, it's not so bad. You get your keep, and it's steady work.'

'But you wouldn't mind earning a little extra—fifty pounds, say?'

'Fifty pounds!' It was as much as Vince could do to imagine such a huge amount of money.

Palmerdale moved closer and spoke in a confidential whisper. 'I need to send an urgent message to London. I assume you know how to use the telegraph?'

Vince nodded. 'Ben taught me, sir. But it can only be used for official business. Strict rule, that is.'

Palmerdale believed firmly that every man had his price. If the first offer was refused, you simply increased the size of the bribe. He pulled a wad of notes from his pocket, and riffled them persuasively under Vince's nose. 'Look, when I say fifty pounds, I mean fifty pounds now. It's all I happen to be carrying. There'll be another fifty pounds for you, as soon as I get back to London.'

Skinsale came quietly up the stairs and looked into the lamp room. He took in the scene at a glance; Palmerdale's low persuasive voice, the wad of money in his hand, Vince listening as if hypnotised.

There was a big streak of caution in Vince—no one gave you money for nothing. 'I don't want to get mixed up in nothing wrong, sir. It's a fortune, a hundred pounds.'

'Not to a man like me,' boasted Palmerdale. 'See here, my lad.' He thrust his hand under his shirt, fumbled with a hidden fastening, and brought out a handful of gleaming stones. 'Diamonds, worth thousands of pounds. I call 'em my insurance. That's the kind of man I am. You'll get your money, never fear.' He put the diamonds away, and held out the money. 'Here, take it. I'm a businessman. How could there be anything wrong?'

In the shadows of the staircase, Skinsale's face was cold and hard. He'd underestimated Palmerdale's persistence. Something would have to be done.

Something was moving up the outside of the lighthouse. It was shapeless, glowing, and it slithered up the smooth stone walls, higher and higher until it was just beneath the high gallery of the lamp room. There, it waited . . .

Palmerdale scribbled in a leather-covered notebook with a silver pencil. He tore out the page and handed it to Vince. 'Here's the message, it's in my private business code . . .'

They heard the Doctor's cheerful voice. 'Vince! Are you up there?'

Palmerdale put a finger to his lips. 'Send the message as soon as you get a chance. And remember, say nothing to anyone. I'll step out on the gallery until the Doctor's gone.'

Palmerdale slipped out on to the darkened gallery. Vince stuffed money and message into his pocket and gave a hasty blast on the foghorn, just as the Doctor entered.

'Are you all right, Vince? We've left you alone up here for quite a time.'

'I'm right enough, sir,' said Vince. But his face was white, and his voice quivered with nerves.

The Doctor put a hand on his shoulder. 'Good lad. Now then, I've got something important to tell you . . .'

Harker found tools and some old lumber in a corner of the coal store. He chopped a plank into a number of rough wedges, and hammered them into place around the edges of the main door. He drove the last one home just as Leela came in. 'There, that should do the trick, eh, miss?'

Leela was chanting, 'Keep the boipressure up keep the boipressure up . . .' Somehow her message had got a bit garbled on the way.

'What's that, again, miss?'

'It is a message from the Doctor. The old one Reuben is not listening, so you must keep the boipressure up.'

'Ah,' said Harker thoughtfully. 'Would that be boiler-pressure, now?'

'That is what I said.'

' 'Course it is, miss. Tell the Doctor not to worry, I'll see to it.'

Harker found the shovel and began shovelling coal into the boiler.

Leela picked up the hammer Harker had been using. She hefted it thoughtfully and slipped from the room.

The Doctor was engaged in the difficult task of putting Vince on his guard without scaring him to death. He told him of the cry from the generator room, and Reuben's strange behaviour.

Vince's eyes widened with terror. 'What do you reckon Reuben saw then, Doctor?'

'I don't know yet. But I think we'll find out before sunrise.'

'It's the Beast come back,' said Vince fearfully. 'Last time they found two keepers dead, and one mad with fear. Well, Ben's dead, isn't he, and Reuben's mad ... Only me left now ...' He clutched the Doctor's arm. 'It'll come for me next!'

'That's superstitious nonsense, Vince.'

'Is it? Look what happened to Ben—and now Reuben!'

'Whatever happened all those years ago, Vince, things are very different now. There's something dangerous on the rock, I don't deny. But there are eight of us here now, Vince. If it attacks again, we'll all be ready and waiting. All the advantages are with us. Remember, it's eight to one!'

The glowing shape paused underneath the gallery, gathering its strength. Its glow pulsed, then grew steadily brighter.

Coat collar turned up round his neck, Palmerdale shivered in the darkness of the gallery. Inside the lamp room, he could see the Doctor talking earnestly to Vince. Would the fellow never shut up and go away? He considered going back into the lamp room. What did it matter if the Doctor saw him? Vince had been well paid, he'd keep his mouth shut. Still, better not to arouse any curiosity. He decided to hang on for a little longer.

Lord Palmerdale put his hands on the guard-rail and peered out into the darkness. Still this confounded fog. He noticed a strange greenish glow from somewhere below him. A kind of phosphorescence ... He leaned over the guard-rail to get a better look—and a glowing tentacle whipped up from out of the darkness and took him round the neck.

Palmerdale went rigid, mouth distorted in a silent scream. Blue lightning flashed round his body as the tentacle snatched him over the guard-rail.

The glowing shape slid down the tower, towards an open window just below.

Skinsale and Adelaide were locked in furious argument. Skinsale had begun it, apparently quite deliberately. On his return to the crew room he had began making a series of disparaging remarks about Lord Palmerdale. Although Adelaide was prepared to admit to herself that his lordship's manners left much to be desired, he was a generous employer, and she felt obliged to come to his defence.

'You've no right to say such things. Lord Palmerdale is the kindest and most considerate of men.'

'To you no doubt,' sneered Skinsale. 'My experience has been somewhat different.'

'You've enjoyed his friendship—and the financial advantages of your association with him. I happen to know he has been most generous . . .'

'A sprat to catch a mackerel! He plans to make far more money out of me than I ever had from him.'

'Indeed?' said Adelaide loftily. 'We both know that Lord Palmerdale is already a millionaire. How could you bring him any financial advantage?'

'He plied me with drink, encouraged me to gamble until I was almost ruined, then persuaded me to give him secret government information, information which he can turn to profit. Your precious employer is a crook and a skunk, my dear!'

'How dare you!' stormed Adelaide. 'I refuse to listen to another word. I shall go and find his lordship and tell him what a perfidious so-called friend you are.'

'Yes, somehow I thought you might,' said Skinsale

softly. With a smile of satisfaction he watched Adelaide run from the room.

Leela marched determinedly up to Reuben's door, the heavy coal hammer over her shoulder. The trouble with the Doctor, she thought, was that he was too considerate. If the old man had information they needed, then he must come out and give it to them.

She came to a halt outside Reuben's door. 'Old one, hear me,' she shouted. 'If you do not open this door now I shall smash it down. Do you understand?'

Silence. Leela stepped back and raised the hammer.

The Doctor clapped Vince encouragingly on the shoulder. 'So, Harker will keep the boiler stoked, you look after the light and keep the siren going, and I'll organise the others to keep watch.'

'All right, Doctor, if you think that's best. You're sure it'd be no good me having a word with Reuben?'

'No good at all, Vince. You stay here, you've got your job to do.'

A splintering crash came from below. They listened. The crash came again, and again. 'Stay here,' ordered the Doctor. 'I'll go down and take a look.'

*

The door to Reuben's room was made of solid oak, and for all her efforts Leela was unable to smash it down. However, by hammering at the same spot, she managed to bash a hole in it. She peered through it, and saw Reuben standing motionless in the middle of the room. His face was white, his eyes stared blankly ahead.

Leela shouted through the gap. 'Come out, old one!' Reuben ignored her.

She stepped back, raising the hammer for another swing. She was about to bring it smashing down when a hand caught the hammer just below the head and held it still. The Doctor had come up behind her. 'That'll be quite enough of that, Leela.'

'You do not want the old one?'

The Doctor peered through the hole. 'He'll come out when he's ready. He's in a kind of coma at the moment. He probably couldn't tell us much, even if we did get him out.'

They heard agitated footsteps behind them, and saw Adelaide running towards them. 'Have you seen Lord Palmerdale? I've looked everywhere for him. I thought he might have come up here to rest.'

The Doctor shook his head. 'Old Reuben's locked himself in his room, and there's nobody in the lamp room except young Vince.' He took Adelaide by the shoulders and turned her round. 'Get back to the crew room.'

'But I must find Lord Palmerdale,' protested Adelaide.

'Get back to the crew room,' repeated the Doctor firmly.

Somewhat to her own surprise, Adelaide turned and walked meekly away.

The Doctor looked at the battered door and shook his head. 'Malicious damage to a lighthouse! That's a very serious business, Leela!'

When the Doctor left the lamp room Vince waited for a few minutes and then went to the gallery door. 'He's gone, sir. You can come in now.'

There was no answer. 'Your lordship?' Thinking Palmerdale must be on the other side, Vince walked right round the gallery, ending up back where he'd started.

Lord Palmerdale was gone. In total amazement, Vince stared down into the darkness.

9

The Chameleon Factor

Vince gave a gasp of horror and ran back into the lamp room. Palmerdale had gone over the edge—and he had a bundle of his lordship's money in his pocket. They'd say he'd robbed him and pushed him over. He tugged the roll of five-pound notes from his pocket, crumpled them up on the floor. He screwed up Palmerdale's code message and put it with the money, struck a match with shaking hands and set light to the little heap of paper.

It was more money than he'd ever see again in his lifetime—but there was nothing but relief in Vince's heart as he watched it burn.

The Doctor and Leela found Skinsale and Adelaide in the crew room. They were sat with their backs to each other, ostentatiously not talking. The Doctor said, 'Ask Harker to come up here, Leela, and then see if you can find Lord Palmerdale.'

'The fat cowardly one?'

'That's right!'

Leela moved silently away, and the Doctor turned

to the others. 'Now then, I want to have a little talk with you two.'

'Really, Doctor,' drawled Skinsale. 'What about?'

'Survival, Colonel. Yours, mine, all of us here on this lighthouse.'

'You're not still worried about this mysterious sea-beast that eats lighthouse keepers?'

'You find the idea of such a creature hard to accept, Colonel?'

'Come now, Doctor, we're both men of intelligence and education . . .'

'Quite so, Colonel. I don't believe in Reuben's sea monster either.'

'Then why do you consistently suggest we are in danger?'

The Doctor said calmly, 'Somewhere out there is an intelligent, hostile alien from a distant planet. I believe it intends to destroy us all.'

An unbelieving smile spread over Skinsale's face. 'An intelligent, hostile alien from a distant planet?'

Adelaide was equally scornful. 'That is the most ridiculous suggestion I have ever heard in my life. And you are supposed to be a scientist!'

Leela appeared with Harker close behind her. 'I cannot find the cowardly one, Doctor.'

The Doctor nodded, and went on trying to convince Skinsale. 'I've never been more serious in my life, Colonel. We're facing an enemy with greater powers than you can imagine.'

Skinsale rose and stretched. 'My dear Doctor, I

too enjoy the scientific romances of Mr Wells but——'

'Old Herbert George may get a few of his facts wrong, but his basic supposition is sound enough!' said the Doctor heatedly. 'Do you really think your little speck in the galaxy is the only one with intelligent life?'

He was interrupted by a blast from the voice-pipe. The Doctor picked it up, listened for a moment and said, 'All right, stay where you are.' He put back the tube. 'That was young Vince. He says Lord Palmerdale has fallen from the lamp gallery.'

Adelaide let out a piercing shriek and immediately Leela slapped her face.

Skinsale said, 'Fallen? But you *can't* fall, there's a perfectly good safety-rail.'

The Doctor nodded. 'I quite agree. But Vince says he was on the gallery, and now he's gone. The question is, do we go outside to look for him?'

Skinsale studied the Doctor's grim face. 'You really believe in this—alien, don't you?'

'Yes, I do. Leela, stay here and look after Adelaide.'

The Doctor, Harker and Skinsale moved off. As they went down the stairs, they didn't realise that Reuben was watching them from the stairway above. His face was twisted, and his dead eyes stared glassily down at them.

*

93

Leela stood warily by the door, while Adelaide sobbed quietly in her chair. 'I told Lord Palmerdale we shouldn't come, but he wouldn't listen. He laughed when I told him Miss Nethercott had seen danger in the stars. I knew something ghastly would happen. Her predictions are never wrong.'

'Your stars?' said Leela. 'Ah, I understand. She is your shaman.'

'My astrologer,' corrected Adelaide. 'I consult her regularly and——'

'A waste of time,' interrupted Leela. 'I too used to believe in magic, but that was before the Doctor taught me about science. It is better to believe in science.'

Harker knocked out the wedges and they all went outside, with lanterns, making a circuit of the lighthouse. It didn't take them long to find Palmerdale's body, lying at the base of the tower. They picked the body up and carried it into the generator room.

While Harker began knocking the wedges back into place, the Doctor and Skinsale carried the body upstairs to the crew room, and laid it on a bunk. Adelaide gave a cry of horror. 'Be quiet,' ordered Leela. 'Have you never seen death before?'

'I can't bear it,' sobbed Adelaide.

Skinsale patted her awkwardly on the back. 'Now, be brave, my dear.'

'Keep away from me!' she screamed. 'You did this. You pushed him over!'

'Don't be ridiculous!'

'You went out of this room after him, not long ago. You followed him to the gallery, and pushed him over.'

'I was never even in the lamp room, let alone the gallery,' protested Skinsale. 'It's true I followed him, but only to see what he was up to!'

'You did it, I know you did it,' screamed Adelaide. 'You killed him!' She began to sob hysterically.

Leela raised a threatening hand. 'Enough!'

Adelaide fell into a chair and buried her face in her hands.

The Doctor looked up from his examination of Palmerdale's body. 'And what was his lordship up to?'

'He was bribing that young keeper to send a message—.'

'So you came back down here and wrecked the telegraph!' The Doctor pointed to the Morse apparatus. It was smashed beyond all chance of repair, wiring ripped out, telegraph key wrenched off.

'It was the only way I could think of to stop him,' admitted Skinsale. 'I'd have been dishonoured, ruined, if he'd got that message out.'

'So to protect your precious honour you put all our lives in danger.'

Suddenly Adelaide realised what the Doctor meant. 'There's no way of contacting the mainland!'

'None at all. We're on our own now.'

Harker hammered the last wedge back into place and straightened up. Sensing that there was someone behind him, he turned. Reuben was standing at the bottom of the stairs.

Poor old fellow looked terrible, thought Harker. With that white skin and those glaring eyes he seemed scarcely human. Best try to get him back to bed. 'Hullo, shipmate,' he said soothingly. 'How are you feeling then?'

Reuben's face twisted into a ghastly smile, as he shuffled slowly towards Harker, hands outstretched . . .

Pacing nervously about the lamp room, Vince recollected guiltily that he hadn't sounded the siren for quite some time. He tugged at the lever. The booming note rang out—then died away in a kind of tired bleat . . .

The Doctor resumed his examination of Palmerdale's body and Skinsale began talking earnestly to Adelaide. 'I swear to you, I didn't harm him.'

'Then who did?'

'I don't know. Could have been Harker, I suppose.

He blamed Henry for losing the ship, actually attacked him earlier.'

'Oh, that's absurd.'

'Is it? No more absurd than saying that I murdered him.'

The Doctor straightened up. 'I almost wish you had, Colonel—it would all be so simple then. Unfortunately he was dead before he hit the ground. Lord Palmerdale was killed by a massive electric shock. Ben, the engineer, died in exactly the same way.'

'Electrocuted on the lamp gallery?' said Skinsale incredulously.

The Doctor nodded. 'While Vince was in the lamp room—I was there myself part of the time.'

'But it's not possible, Doctor. That would mean this—creature can climb sheer walls.'

'It can do considerably more than that, Colonel. It's amphibious, it has a natural affinity with electricity and it has the technological ability to adapt its environment. Do you follow me?'

'No,' said Skinsale frankly. 'Not a word, Doctor.'

'It likes the cold. Not enough data yet to place the species—but heat could be a useful method of defence.'

The voice-pipe whistled and Leela went to answer it. She listened then said urgently, 'Doctor, Vince says the boipressure has fallen—and the siren will not sound.'

'Harker,' said the Doctor. He set off at a run, and the others followed.

They found Harker's body sprawled by the generator. The Doctor knelt beside it, the others crowding into the room behind him. Adelaide caught sight of the body and started to scream again. 'Get her out of here,' said the Doctor impatiently. Skinsale hurried her away.

Leela looked at the body. 'He is like the others?'

The Doctor nodded. He rose slowly then looked at the door. Harker's wedges were still all in place. The Doctor stood thinking for a moment. He went over to the coal store, flung open the door and went inside. A moment later he emerged, dragging Reuben's body. He bent and tried to flex an arm. It was as stiff as an iron bar. 'Rigor mortis. He's been dead for hours.'

'Hours, Doctor? That's impossible. Less than an hour ago, Harker saw him go upstairs. I saw him standing in his room.'

'You saw something, Leela. But it wasn't Reuben. He was lying dead down here all the time.'

'But I saw him . . .'

The Doctor's face was grim. 'Shape changing, Leela. Sometimes called the chameleon factor. Several species have developed it, and our alien must belong to one of them.' He looked at the door, still firmly barred by Harker's wedges. 'I've made a terrible mistake, Leela. I thought I'd locked the enemy out. Instead, I've locked it in here—with us!'

10

The Rutan

Vince tried the siren foghorn again, but it gave only the faintest of moans. He wondered vaguely why Harker didn't get on with stoking the boilers.

There was a dragging footstep from the doorway. He saw Reuben shuffling slowly towards him. Vince was shocked by the old man's ghastly appearance. 'You shouldn't be out of bed, Reuben. Don't you worry about me, I'll hang on here till morning. You get some rest.'

Reuben said nothing. His face twisted in a horrible parody of a grin as he lurched slowly forward, arms reaching out.

Alarmed, Vince started to back away. 'Reuben, what's wrong? No, Reuben . . . No . . .'

Reuben lunged forward with terrifying speed, and grabbed Vince's shoulders. Immediately Vince went rigid, and blue sparks arced around his body.

Working at frantic speed, the Doctor shovelled in all the coal the boiler would hold. 'Don't want the lights failing now, do we?' He closed the boiler doors, and checked the pressure gauges.

'This alien has great powers, Doctor. To change its shape at will . . .'

'Yes, it has . . . though first it needed to analyse the human life pattern.'

'That is why it stole the body of the engineer?'

'That's right. After that it was simply a matter of organic restructuring. Elementary biology for Time Lords.'

'But if the creature is a Time Lord, there is nothing we can do.'

'I didn't mean it was a Time Lord,' explained the Doctor patiently. 'Certainly not! But elementary biology for us is something a lesser species might master—after a few thousand centuries or so.'

Leela swung from despair to total confidence. 'Then we have nothing to worry about.'

'We don't? That's nice to hear.'

'You will easily dispose of this primitive creature.'

'I will?'

'Of course. After all, you are a Time Lord!'

'I admire your confidence,' said the Doctor ruefully. 'You know, it must have taken Reuben's form for a reason.'

'So that it could kill us stealthily, one by one! Doctor, suppose we pretend that we think Reuben is still Reuben and not the alien . . . could we not get close to it and kill it?'

'No, no, Leela. If we get close to it, then it gets close to us. Once it gets within touching distance, we're dead. It packs too many volts.' The Doctor was prowling thoughtfully around the generator. Suddenly he dropped to the ground, and reached under the machine. 'Aha, I thought so!'

'What is it?'

The Doctor got up and held out a complicated-looking metallic spiral of strange and alien design. 'It's a power relay!'

'It was placed there by the alien?'

'Of course! Rule One, on surviving a crash landing, send up some kind of distress beacon. Its ship was damaged so it needed another power-source.' The Doctor tapped the generator. 'That's why it came here. There must be a signal modulator as well, probably somewhere higher up the tower. That will be transmitting the actual message. I've got to find it . . . Leela, you take the others up to the lamp room.'

'Why there?'

'It's the easiest place to defend.'

'Then we look for this . . . mognal sigulator?'

'I'll do the looking. Now hurry, we haven't much time.'

Adelaide sat hunched by the dying fire while Skinsale paced nervously about the crew room. 'Oh, do keep still,' she snapped.

Skinsale looked at her in surprise. 'I'm sorry,' she said hastily. 'It's just that I'm so frightened. This is all like some terrible dream.'

'Pity it's not, we might stand some chance of waking up!' Skinsale turned as Leela came into the room. 'I suppose Harker's dead too?'

Leela nodded. 'Yes, like the others.'

Adelaide jumped to her feet, opening her mouth to scream. Leela glared warningly at her. 'There is no time for weeping. The creature has got into the lighthouse. Now we must fight for our lives—and everyone must play their part.'

Adelaide fainted.

When the Doctor arrived outside the little cabin, Reuben's door was standing open. He slipped into the empty room and began a rapid search. Even without the power relay, the signal modulator would transmit for some time. It was essential to find and destroy it.

The room was tiny and the Doctor's search thorough—but he found nothing. Suddenly he heard slow dragging footsteps coming along the corridor. Immediately he switched off the lights and looked for a hiding place. But the room was too small— there was nowhere to go.

The creature in Reuben's shape came along the landing and paused on the threshold as if sensing danger. It came into the room and switched on the light, looking round suspiciously. The room was empty. It moved over to the window and drew the curtain.

Outside the window, the Doctor was plastered flat against the sheer side of the lighthouse, high above the rocky ground. His toes were on a tiny ledge and his fingers clasped a shallow ridge between the stone blocks. He clung to the side of the lighthouse like a fly on the wall. All at once the Doctor saw a glint of alien metal just above the window ledge. He had found the signal modulator. Suddenly he felt his fingers beginning to slip and wondered how much longer he could hold on . . .

Leela watched impatiently as Skinsale held a glass of water to Adelaide's lips. 'Drink this, Adelaide. Come along, drink it.'

'Hurry,' snapped Leela. 'The Doctor wants us to go to the lamp room?'

'Why the lamp room?'

'He says it is the easiest place to defend. If she cannot walk then we must carry her.'

Skinsale helped Adelaide to rise. 'Come along now.'

She clung to him in blind panic. 'No . . . no . . .'

Skinsale lifted Adelaide to her feet and half carried her towards the door. There was a dragging footstep outside the room and Leela shouted, 'Back! Get back!'

Reuben appeared in the doorway. He stared at

them for a moment. His white face twisted in a ghastly smile.

The Doctor heard Reuben leave the little room, and started edging his way slowly towards the window. He reached it at last, heaving a great sigh of relief when his feet were on the sill. He rested for a moment and then reached upwards, wrenched the signal modulator from its niche in the stonework and climbed thankfully back into the room.

Leela, Skinsale and Adelaide backed away as Reuben advanced slowly towards them, the horrible grimace still fixed on his deathly-white face.

The monster sprang with terrifying speed, choosing Adelaide for its target. It clasped her in its arms in a deadly embrace. Her back arched, she went rigid and blue sparks flamed round her body.

Leela snatched the knife from her boot and hurled it with all her strength. It struck the monster's chest and rebounded harmlessly.

The monster's lunge for Adelaide had left clear the path to the doorway. 'Run!' shouted Leela, and fled up the stairs. Skinsale hesitated for an agonised moment and then followed.

The Reuben creature let go of Adelaide, who slumped lifeless to the floor.

*

The Doctor, Leela and Skinsale collided on the stairs. 'The creature is close behind us,' panted Leela. 'We must find weapons.'

'I know,' said the Doctor calmly. He gripped Skinsale by his arm. 'Listen carefully, Colonel. Just below the lamp room is the service room. It's full of maroons and rockets. I want you to break them open and scatter the powder on the lamp-room steps. Have you got that?'

Skinsale nodded. 'Right, Doctor, leave it to me.'

There was a dragging footstep on the stair. 'It's coming,' called Leela.

The Doctor gave her a shove. 'Off you go, then, both of you!'

Leela and Skinsale dashed away.

The Doctor stood waiting.

The Reuben creature came slowly onwards. It stopped when it saw the Doctor, as if sensing a trap.

'Can I help you?' said the Doctor politely. 'You don't look very well. Are you having trouble? Not too easy holding the human form for so long, is it?'

The creature spoke, but its voice was not that of Reuben. It was weird, high, shrill, totally alien. 'It is no longer necessary. We can now abandon this unpleasantly primitive shape.'

'Why don't you do that?' suggested the Doctor. 'You'll find it much comfier, I'm sure.'

Reuben's body began to glow and melt and change . . . The human form warped and twisted and finally disappeared. In its place was a glowing shapeless mass. The creature was resuming its natural form.

Leela and Skinsale dashed into the lamp room, their arms full of rockets and maroons, and immediately stumbled over Vince's body. Skinsale examined it. 'Dead, like all the others.'

'Then there is nothing we can do,' said Leela practically. 'Let us move the body out of the way and then prepare the weapons.'

Skinsale was staring at Vince's body. The sudden spate of violent deaths had shaken him badly. 'That ghastly creature plans to kill us all—just like poor Vince . . .'

'You must forget him now,' said Leela practically. 'Now it is time for us to fight!'

A shrill alien howl came from below.

The howl was the triumphant cry of the alien, now back in its natural shape. The Doctor, who had been watching the transformation with detached scientific interest, was able to see the true shape of his enemy at last.

To be frank, he thought, it wasn't a pretty sight. In place of Reuben's form there was a huge, dimly glowing gelatinous mass, internal organs pulsing gently inside the semi-transparent body. Somewhere near the centre were huge many-faceted eyes, and a shapeless orifice that could have been a mouth. The

Doctor nodded. 'Well, well, well, I should have guessed. Reuben the Rutan, eh?'

'We are a Rutan scout, specially trained in the newly-developed shape-shifting techniques.' (Rutans have little concept of individual identity, seeing themselves as units of the all-conquering Rutan race. Hence they always speak in the plural.)

'Never mind,' said the Doctor consolingly. 'I expect you'll get better with practice. What are you doing in this part of the galaxy, anyway?'

'That does not concern you. You are to be destroyed.'

'Got it. You're losing that interminable war of yours with the Sontarans.'

The Sontaran–Rutan war had raged through the cosmos for untold centuries. An insane struggle to the death between two fiercely militaristic species, it had swept to and fro over hundreds of planets, first one side winning and then the other. 'I should have realised I was dealing with a Rutan,' thought the Doctor. But they were a strange savage species with an implacable hatred for all life-forms other than their own. Even the Sontarans were preferable —and that was saying something!

The Doctor's charge provoked a fierce crackle of rage from the Rutan. 'That is a lie!'

'Is it? You used to hold the whole of Mutters Spiral once. Now the Sontarans must have driven you to the far fringes of the galaxy.'

'The glorious Rutan Army is making a planned

series of strategic withdrawals to selected strong-points . . .'

'That's the empty rhetoric of a defeated dictator-ship, Rutan,' mocked the Doctor. 'And I don't like your face either!'

'Your mockery will end with your race, Earthling, when the mighty Rutan Battle Fleet occupies this planet.'

Suddenly the Doctor realised that the fate of the whole Earth was at stake in this struggle. 'Why bother to invade a planet like Earth? It's of no poss-ible value to you.'

'The planet is obscure, but its strategic position is sound. We shall use it as a launch-point for our final assault on the Sontarans.'

'If you set up a power-base here, the Sontarans will bombard the planet with photonic missiles. Be-tween the two of you, you'll destroy the earth in your struggle.'

'That is unimportant. The sacrifice of the planet will serve the cause of the final glorious Rutan vic-tory!'

'And what about its people?'

'Primitive bipeds of no value. We have scouted all the planets of this solar system. Only this one is suit-able for our purpose.'

The Doctor had a ghastly vision of Earth as the battlefield in a vast interplanetary conflict. Who-ever won, the people of Earth would lose. 'I can understand your military purpose. But why are you bothering to murder a handful of harmless people?'

'It is necessary. Until we return to our Mother Ship, and the Mother Ship informs the Fleet that a suitable planet has been found, no one must know of our visit to Earth.'

'But you crashed, didn't you, Rutan? Just as you made your discovery. You've failed.'

'We are sending a signal to the Mother Ship, with the power from the primitive mechanism below.'

'You're not, you know.' The Doctor tossed the gleaming alien spiral down the stairs.

There was a crackle of anger. 'It is of no importance. The Ship will still home in on the primary signal.'

The Doctor threw the larger spiral after the first. 'I'm sorry to disappoint you, but I fixed that too!'

'All your interference is useless. The beam was transmitting long enough for the Mother Ship to trace the signal and fix our position.'

The Rutan was probably quite right, thought the Doctor. But he refused to admit defeat. 'You can't be sure of that, can you—oyster-face?'

There was total confidence in the Rutan's voice. 'The Ship will come.'

'Perhaps. But long before that you will be dead!'

'We are Rutan! What could you Earthlings possibly do to harm us?'

'Just step this way and I'll show you,' said the Doctor politely—and sprinted back up the stairs.

Unhurriedly the glowing mass of the Rutan flowed

after him. There was no need for haste. The stairs led only to the lamp room, the highest point of the lighthouse tower. After that there was nowhere to go.

The Doctor was trapped.

11

Ambush

The Doctor ran up the last few stairs, his feet crunching on the thick black powder underfoot. He had managed to delay the Rutan long enough for Leela and Skinsale to do their work. They were waiting for him just inside the lamp-room doorway.

'I've brought someone to see you,' said the Doctor. 'I hope you're ready for visitors, he'll be here any minute. Pass me one of those fuses, Colonel.'

Skinsale passed him the fuse, a short piece of soft rope, frayed at both ends. The Doctor was patting his pockets. 'I'm sorry to bother you,' he said politely. 'Could you oblige me with a light?'

'Yes, of course!' Skinsale produced some matches, lit one and held it to the Doctor's fuse, much as if he were lighting a friend's cigar. 'I say, Doctor, do you really think this is advisable? So much powder in a confined space?'

'Probably not. But we've no other choice.' A faint crackling came from the stairs below. 'I think our guest is coming.'

The crackling grew louder, and a faint greenish glow appeared round the turn of the stairs. 'How did you manage to hold it back for so long?' whispered Leela.

'Just a little military chit-chat. You know what these old soldiers are once they get talking.'

The Rutan moved round the bend of the stairs and came into full view. At the sight of the glowing, pulsating mass, Skinsale gave a gasp of horror, and even Leela took an involuntary pace back. Only the Doctor was unimpressed. 'Ah, there you are. What took you so long?'

'The time for talk is over now,' shrilled the weird, high-pitched voice.

'Correct!' The Doctor threw the fizzing fuse.

It landed close to the Rutan, on the powder-strewn stairway. There was a blinding flash and the stairway disappeared in a sheet of flame. The Rutan sprang back with a high-pitched shriek of agony. When the smoke cleared it had gone.

'Where is it, Doctor?' demanded Leela fiercely. 'Have we killed the thing?'

'Unlikely, I'm afraid!'

Skinsale was sweating with relief. 'I've never seen anything so horrible! What the devil was it?'

'An intelligent, highly-aggressive alien life-form from the planet Ruta 3.'

'Was it a sea-creature?' asked Leela.

'Evolved in the sea, adapted to land. Now then, Colonel, what about some more gunpowder?' Skinsale ran down into the service room.

Leela's eyes were fixed on the stairs. 'We are

lucky that the beast fears the flame, Doctor.'

'Ruta 3 is an icy planet. The inhabitants find heat intensely painful. What we really need is a flame-thrower!'

Skinsale came out of the service room lugging what looked like a small oddly-shaped cannon. 'What about this thing, Doctor? Some sort of mortar by the look of it.'

The Doctor helped Skinsale carry the device up to the lamp-room doorway. 'It's an early Schemurly!' he exclaimed delightedly.

'It's a what?'

The Doctor repeated the tongue-twisting phrase. 'An early Schemurly. It fires a rocket and line.'

'Then we could fire it at the monster.'

'We could, but it wouldn't do any good. Projectile weapons are useless against a Rutan. They go straight through and it simply seals the wound. The only way to dispose of a Rutan is to blow it to bits.'

Skinsale looked nervously at the stairs. 'Then what are we going to do?'

'Stay calm,' said the Doctor. 'I'll see what I can find.' He went dourly into the service room and began rooting through lockers and shelves. A few minutes later he emerged carrying a gun-like device mounted on a tripod. 'Rocket-launcher,' he explained. 'Now, loaded with a few extra odds and ends this could cover the stairs.' The Doctor went over to the tool-locker and came back with an assortment of rusty tins, filled with nuts and bolts, nails, cogs and other engineering debris. He began picking out the biggest and sharpest objects and arranging them in a little pile. 'Mind you,' the Doctor went on, 'it's not just this Rutan I'm concerned about. It's the others.'

Skinsale went pale. 'Others? You mean there are more of the creatures?'

Briefly the Doctor explained the background of the Rutan–Sontaran conflict, and the Rutan plans for Earth. 'By the time the Rutans and Sontarans have finished with it, this planet will be a dead cinder hanging in space.'

'Is there nothing we can do?'

The Doctor considered. 'The Battle Fleet won't come here unless the Rutan Mother Ship reports back with the news that their scout has found a suitable planet. If we could kill the Rutan, and knock out the Mother Ship as well . . . The Rutans are a cautious species. They'd simply conclude that this sector of space was too dangerous.'

'Then that is what we must do,' said Leela firmly. She looked expectantly at the Doctor. 'How?'

'How indeed. We've nothing here that would stop a Rutan spaceship in its tracks . . .' The Doctor struggled to recall what he knew of Rutan technology. 'Rutan ships have a crystalline infrastructure. They're shielded of course, but landing on a primitive planet like this they might risk cutting the protective energy-fields to save power.' The Doctor looked at his two companions, who hadn't understood a word of what he'd said. 'What we really need is an amplified carbon-oscillator.'

Leela frowned. 'Doctor, what exactly is a—whatever-you-said?'

'Something like a laser-beam, but far more destructive.'

Leela struggled to remember the science lectures which the Doctor occasionally delivered during their journeys in the TARDIS.

'A laser . . . that's some kind of very powerful light, isn't it?'

'Well, yes, putting it in the very simplest terms——'

Leela pointed to the lighthouse reflector lamp. 'Then why don't we use this?'

The Doctor stared hard at the lamp and then looked back at Leela. 'You mean convert the carbon-arc beam? Leela, that's a beautiful notion . . .'

'It is?'

The Doctor's face fell. 'Unfortunately I'd need a focusing device. A fairly large chunk of crystalline carbon.'

Skinsale seized eagerly on the first words he'd understood. 'Crystalline carbon? A diamond you mean?'

He held up his wrist and light glinted on his diamond cuff-links.

'Yes, that's right, but I'm afraid those are far too

small. I'd need a fairly large one for the primary beam oscillator.'

'Palmerdale was carrying diamonds. He called them his insurance.'

'Then they'd still be on his body—in the crew room?'

'Yes.'

'Yes,' said the Doctor thoughtfully. 'Well, let's get this rocket-launcher ready first.'

Recovered now from the shock of the searing explosion, the Rutan flowed out of the generator room and up the stairs. It was cautious now, fearing more Earthling attacks, and it moved very slowly.

The Doctor packed the last few nails down the muzzle of the rocket-launcher. 'Right, that should do it. Sure you know how to work it?' Leela nodded and the Doctor rose, 'Then I'll be off.'

Skinsale got up too. 'I'm coming with you.'

'It isn't necessary, you know.'

'I want to. You'll need some help. Two will stand a better chance than one.'

'All right. Remember, Leela, don't fire until you see the green of its tentacles.'

They moved towards the door.

'How will you get past the Rutan?' asked Leela.

'With great discretion,' said the Doctor solemnly. 'With any luck it'll have retreated to the lower levels. Come on, Colonel.'

They crept cautiously down the stairs, past the smoke-blackened area of the explosion. They rounded the turn and came on to the crew-room landing. There was no sign of the Rutan.

The Doctor waved Skinsale forward and they slipped into the deserted crew room—empty except for Adelaide huddled where she had fallen, and the body of Palmerdale on the bunk.

The Doctor stood waiting by the door, waving Skinsale over to the body. Skinsale pulled back the blanket and began searching Palmerdale's pockets. He looked up at the Doctor and shook his head. 'Body-belt?' suggested the Doctor.

Skinsale felt inside Palmerdale's shirt and felt the stiff canvas belt with its pouch. He fumbled with the fastenings, his fingers stiff and clumsy.

The Rutan moved slowly up the staircase, all its senses alert. At the faint sounds of movement from the crew room it paused, and the pulsing glow became brighter as it gathered its energies. Moving faster now, it flowed on up the steps towards the crew-room landing.

Skinsale wrenched open the pouch, clawed out the

handful of diamonds and went to join the Doctor. He tipped the pile of diamonds into the Doctor's cupped hands. The Doctor selected one diamond, the largest and finest, and tossed the rest carelessly on the floor. 'Come on,' he said and hurried off.

Skinsale stared down at the gleaming stones at his feet. There was a fortune there, enough to keep him in comfort for the rest of his life. He couldn't leave them ... Quickly he bent down—and began scrabbling for the gleaming stones.

There was a glow from the stairs as the Rutan flowed on to the landing and sprang forward into the crew room. A tentacle lashed out, curling round Skinsale's body and there was a crackle of blue sparks. Skinsale screamed ...

Just up the stairs the Doctor heard the sound and turned back. He ran down to the landing, looked into the crew room and saw the Rutan clasping its victim. Realising he could do nothing he turned and ran.

The Rutan dropped Skinsale's dead body and flowed after the Doctor with appalling speed. This time it was risking no Earthling traps. It would catch the Doctor and kill him now. Then there would only be the female.

The Doctor shot up the stairs three at a time, the angry crackling of the Rutan close behind him. If it got near enough to reach him with a tentacle he was finished—and so was Earth ...

As the Doctor ran up the last few steps the Rutan was close on his heels. It was almost upon him as he rounded the bend and saw Leela crouched behind the rocket-launcher.

As the Doctor dashed for the lamp-room doorway, the Rutan gathered all its energies for a final effort. With a shrill cry of triumph it sprang . . .

12

The Last Battle

Leela crouched behind the rocket-launcher, frozen with horror. With the Doctor directly in front of her, how could she fire? Yet if she didn't shoot, the Rutan would surely catch him . . .

One tremendous flying leap took the Doctor over the rocket-launcher, and clear over Leela's head.

With the Doctor in mid-air the Rutan surged forward—and Leela fired.

There was an ear-splitting crash as several pounds of assorted ironmongery ripped into the Rutan's body, blasting it back down the staircase.

Leela shook her head, half dazed by the noise. She turned and saw the Doctor sprawled in a heap on the other side of the room. 'Are you all right?'

The Doctor picked himself up, patted himself carefully here and there. 'I think so—you singed the end of my scarf!'

'Where is the Colonel?'

'Dead, I'm afraid.'

'With honour?'

The Doctor hesitated, thinking of Skinsale scrabbling for the diamonds. It was no way for a man to be remembered. 'Yes,' he said firmly. 'With honour.'

'Then we have avenged him. Did you get the diamond?'

The Doctor held out his hand. The pride of Palmerdale's collection was gleaming in his palm.

'I'd better get to work.' The Doctor climbed up to the level of the arc-lamp, feeling for his sonic screwdriver. Soon he was absorbed in dismantling and reassembling the complex machinery. Leela watched him for a moment then went down the stairs. She wanted to be quite sure that their enemy was dead.

She found the Rutan on the landing below, a feebly glowing, jelly-like mass. It crackled faintly at the sight of her, and glowed a little brighter, but it was too weak to do her any harm. Leela called up the stairs. 'It is here, Doctor. I did it. The beast is finished!'

She looked down at the shattered body of her foe.

'Your triumph will be short-lived, Earthling,' whispered the Rutan. 'Soon our Mother Ship will blast this island to molten rock . . .'

'Empty threats, Rutan. Enjoy your death, as I enjoyed killing you!'

The Rutan quivered and pulsed weakly. 'We die for the glory of our race. Long live the Rutan Empire . . .'

The glow faded and died, and the Rutan died with it.

With a savage grin of triumph, Leela turned and went back to the lamp room.

The Doctor had rigged together one of his amazing contraptions, taking apart the reflector lamp and the giant telescope and re-assembling them in an entirely different order. As far as Leela could make out, the power of the carbon-arc lamp would be reflected through the telescope and finally focused through Palmerdale's diamond, which the Doctor was now fitting somewhere inside the telescope. He made a careful, final adjustment and looked up.

'They are hard to kill, these Rutans,' said Leela.

'Been celebrating, have you?'

'Of course. It is fitting to celebrate the death of an enemy.'

'Not in my opinion, but we haven't time to discuss morality. Look over there.'

A streak of light, like a giant fireball, had appeared in the night sky. It was moving steadily towards them . . .

Leela shaded her eyes with her hand. 'Is that the Rutan ship?'

'It is,' said the Doctor grimly. 'Now, I've set this contraption to operate automatically. Once the ship is in range the beam will lock on to its resonator and fire, and we will then have exactly one hundred and seventeen seconds to get clear. Understand?'

'Perfectly!'

'So as soon as I switch on we run for it. All right?'

Leela stared up at the sky. The fireball was approaching with terrifying speed now. It was a moving sun hurtling straight towards them. Its fiery radiance lit up the lamp room like broad daylight, and the throbbing of its power-source grew louder and louder. 'I think you should switch on soon, Doctor. It's getting very near.'

'Nearly ready,' said the Doctor. He snapped a last connection into place and climbed down. The fire-ball was almost on them now. The noise of its approach was deafening, and its radiance hurt the eyes. The Doctor pulled the switch. The rickety-looking set-up began to throb with power . . .

'Come on, Leela. And whatever you do, don't look back!'

The humming of the Doctor's machine blended with the shattering roar of the approaching Rutan spaceship. Leela couldn't resist turning back for a final look. The fireball was so close it seemed about to smash through the lamp-room window. Its brightness almost blinded her . . . The Doctor pulled her towards the stairs. 'I said don't look back. Now run!'

They hurtled down the winding stairs, the Doctor in the lead. Outside the crew room, Leela paused again. She'd lost a good knife in there, when she'd thrown it at the Rutan. It was not good to lose such a fine weapon. She ran into the crew room and looked round.

The Doctor sped on, not realising that Leela was no longer with him. By now the whole lighthouse was shaking with the roar of the Rutan ship's power-source.

Luckily the knife had fallen fairly close to the

door. Leela snatched it up and hurried on.

The Doctor ran down the long flights of stairs, finally reaching the generator room, where the generator was throbbing wildly. The door was still closed, and it took him precious seconds to knock out the wedges with the shovel. He flung the door open —ran outside and suddenly realised he was on his own. 'Leela!' he yelled and ran back into the generator room.

Leela paused to tuck her knife away in her boot, ran down the stairs into the generator room and bumped straight into the Doctor who was just coming in to look for her. He grabbed her wrist and yanked her outside. 'Leela, come on!'

They ran across the little island, slipping and sliding on the wet rocks, and finally flung themselves down behind a jagged rock, not far from where they'd left the TARDIS. By now the whole island was throbbing and shaking with the noise of the Rutan ship's approach.

Leela peeped over the rock. The fireball seemed to be hovering over the lighthouse tower ... A thin beam of light speared out from the tower at the Rutan ship. The fireball glowed brighter and brighter, the noise rose to a screaming crescendo—there was a blinding flash, a colossal explosion, and Leela fell back, her hands over her eyes. The ground convulsed beneath them, and shattered rocks came down from the sky like rain. At last the rumbling echoes of the explosion died away, and all was silent.

The Doctor stood up. The lighthouse was still standing, but the Rutan spaceship had disappeared, blasted to atoms by the force of its own exploding power-drive.

Leela was still crouching down, her hands over her face. Gently he helped her up.

She took her hands from her face and moved her head to and fro. 'Slay me, Doctor!'

'I beg your pardon?' said the Doctor in some astonishment.

'I am blind,' said Leela stoically. 'Slay me now. It is the fate of the old and crippled.'

The Doctor took Leela's face in his hands and stared hard into her eyes. For a moment he looked worried, but then he smiled. 'You're neither old nor crippled, Leela. You were just dazzled by the flash. The effect will pass.'

'You're sure?'

'Yes. Just blink!'

Leela blinked rapidly several times. A hazy shape appeared before her eyes. It cleared, became the Doctor looking down at her. She noticed that he was staring into her eyes.

'That's strange!' he said.

'What is?'

'Pigmentation dispersal caused by the flash.' Leela looked at him in alarm and the Doctor said, 'It's all right. It just means your eyes have changed colour. You can stop blinking now, Leela. It's time to go.'

As they walked towards the TARDIS, Leela asked

curiously, 'What colour are my eyes now?'

'Blue,' said the Doctor. 'Don't worry, it looks very nice.'

She turned for a last look at the lighthouse. 'Doctor, what will the people of this time say about all this? What will they think happened here?'

The Doctor shrugged. 'Who knows? Someone will probably write a poem about it. "Aye though we hunted high and low, and hunted everywhere" . . .'

'What litany is that?'

The Doctor smiled. 'The Ballad of Flannen Isle. Wilfred Gibson.' He opened the TARDIS door.

> ' "Aye, though we hunted high and low,
>   And hunted everywhere,
>   Of the three men's fate we found no trace
>   Of any kind, in any place,
>   But a door ajar, and an untouched meal
>   And an overtoppled chair . . ." '

The Doctor ushered Leela into the TARDIS, followed her and closed the door behind them.

There was a wheezing groaning noise, and the TARDIS vanished. The only sound was the thundering of the waves as they crashed on the jagged coastline of Fang Rock . . .

No one was left alive to hear them.

116151	Terrance Dicks & Malcom Hulke **THE MAKING OF DOCTOR WHO**	60p
114558	Terrance Dicks **DOCTOR WHO AND THE ABOMINABLE SNOWMAN**	40p
116313	Ian Marter **DOCTOR WHO AND THE ARK IN SPACE**	50p
112954	Terrance Dicks **DOCTOR WHO AND THE AUTON INVASION** (illus)	40p
116747	Terrance Dicks **DOCTOR WHO AND THE BRAIN OF MORBIUS**	50p*
110250	Terrance Dicks **DOCTOR WHO AND THE CARNIVAL OF MONSTERS**	50p
11471X	Malcolm Hulke **DOCTOR WHO AND THE CAVE MONSTERS**	40p
117034	Terrance Dicks **DOCTOR WHO AND THE CLAWS OF AXOS**	50p*
113160	David Whitaker **DOCTOR WHO AND THE CRUSADERS** (illus)	40p
114981	Brian Hayles **DOCTOR WHO AND THE CURSE OF PELADON**	40p
114639	Gerry Davis **DOCTOR WHO AND THE CYBERMEN**	40p
113322	Barry Letts **DOCTOR WHO AND THE DAEMONS** (illus)	40p
112873	David Whitaker **DOCTOR WHO AND THE DALEKS**	60p
118421	Terrance Dicks **DOCTOR WHO DINOSAUR BOOK**	75p
112601	Terrance Dicks **DOCTOR WHO AND THE GENESIS OF THE DALEKS**	60p

N.B. 'Doctor Who' Books are published by arrangement with the British Broadcasting Corporation.

†For sale in Britain and Ireland only.
*Not for sale in Canada.

Wyndham Books are obtainable from many booksellers and newsagents. If you have any difficulty please send purchase price plus postage on the scale below to:

Wyndham Cash Sales
P.O. Box 11
Falmouth
Cornwall

While every effort is made to keep prices low, it is sometimes necessary to increase prices at short notice. Wyndham Books reserve the right to show new retail prices on covers which may differ from those advertised in the text or elsewhere.

Postage and Packing Rate

UK: 22p for the first book, plus 10p per copy for each additional book ordered to a maximum charge of 82p. **BFPO and Eire:** 22p for the first book, plus 10p per copy for the next 6 books and thereafter 4p per book. **Overseas:** 30p for the first book and 10p per copy for each additional book.

These charges are subject to Post Office charge fluctuations.